BEHIND THE BLUE ELEVATOR

FELICIA BAXLEY

Copyright © 2021 by Felicia Baxley.

All rights reserved. No part of this publication may be reproduced, distributed or transmitted in any form or by any means, including photocopying, recording, or other electronic or mechanical methods, without the prior written permission of the publisher, except in the case of brief quotations embodied in critical reviews and certain other noncommercial uses permitted by copyright law. For permission requests, write to the publisher, addressed "Attention: Permissions Coordinator," at the address below.

Hustle Write Publications LLC

www.HustleWritePublication.com

Editting Credit: Tam Jernigan (PublisherChick Editing)

Ordering Information:

Quantity sales. Special discounts are available on quantity purchases by corporations, associations, and others. For details, email info@hustlewritepublication.com.

ISBN 978-1-735410-1-0

DEDICATION

This book is dedicated to my amazing mother, Lisa Baxley. Thank you for encouraging me to be the best version of myself. You are my biggest support, and I love you.

DISCLAIMER

Topics of suicide are portrayed and discussed throughout this work of fiction. If these topics trigger you, reconsider reading this work or read in the presence of a trusted loved one.

If you are suffering from suicidal thoughts please reach out to the National Suicide Hotline at (800) 273-8255, or visit suicidepreventionlifeline.org

ONE

Finally, the final semester of senior year started rolling. Even though I still had many years of schooling left for my doctorate, I couldn't help but bask in the accomplishment of making it to that moment. I had landed an internship at a local mental hospital, "Henry Ellin Asylum." It wasn't the internship I had expected, but it was what I was offered, and I was ready to get it done. I would be that much closer to my degree. I can't pretend that it wasn't disappointing to intern in an establishment so far from what I desired, but that was okay. Luckily, I was never opposed to doing community service type deeds. Not to mention, I thought it would give me more experience with seeing different diagnosis. Where else could I really get firsthand exposure to diagnosed patients? What better place than the asylum, right?

"Hi! I'm Ella, I was supposed to start an internship here today." My eagerness caused my voice to come out in almost a high-pitched squeal.

"Sign here." She said tossing a clipboard across the desk, not bothering to look up at me. I snatched my hand back quickly, almost hitting myself in the chest to keep from being smacked with the clipboard.

I rolled my eyes and signed the old broken clipboard under the "Visitor" tab listed at the top. As if queued, the desk lady slapped a dingy "Intern" badge on the desk. "Go down to the automatic doors, use this to badge in, take the first left and go through to the last room on the left," her tone was dry and unenthusiastic.

I didn't bother to acknowledge her other than taking the badge and going on my way with her instructions. While I was eager to start my internship, I could already confirm this wasn't going to be anything like the internship I really wanted. I hadn't had much coffee, and the lack of personality from the desk lady was bleak. I was never one to fake pleasantries with someone who clearly wasn't pleasant.

I was terrible with directions, so I tried my best to remember what she had said. I kept walking in the direction I thought I remembered. She had rubbed me the wrong way and the last thing I planned to do was go back and ask her to repeat herself.

Through the large automatic doors, I found myself walking down a long corridor. "What did she say?" I asked myself. I was trying hard to remember the next direction the she had given me when I realized on one side of the corridor was a large white room behind a glass window the length of the wall. I assume that was some sort of community area for the patients. I found myself watching in awe and amazement. There weren't many patients there, but the few that were I couldn't help but study. I found myself trying to diagnose them, trying to see if I could observe any behaviors that would give me an insight into who they were or what they struggled with.

There weren't any caretakers, at least none that I could see. I scanned the room. There was a woman with frazzled hair in a chair facing a small TV. It didn't seem like she was watching it, more as if she were having a conversation with it. Maybe she was talking with herself. She kept looking behind her, almost as if she wanted to make sure no one was there to hear the intimate things she said in her own ear. She would then turn back around and whisper into her shoulder.

Not too far from her seated in a corner was a younger guy. His hair was shaved close to his scalp. He wasn't as fidgety as the girl. He was actually quite still. If I hadn't been paying close attention, I may have missed him completely. I started straining my eyes because it looked as

ONE

if he was drooling. I couldn't help but wonder if he had a condition or if it was a side effect of the medication he was probably on.

I was still observing the young man when something caught my attention. There was a very handsome middle-aged man sitting at a table. He seemed to be playing cards with himself. He looked very well maintained, especially compared to the other two individuals in the room. I don't know what was so intriguing about him. Maybe the mysteriousness of him being in that room, seemingly out of place. Maybe it was how attractive he was. I really couldn't put my finger on it. I wasn't even totally sure if he was a patient or an orderly. Regardless, there was something intriguing about him. Something that captured my attention. I had completely forgotten about the other two patients in that room. In that moment, he had all of my attention.

As if he could hear my thoughts, he slowly glanced up at me, smiling. Wow! His smile was beautiful. Should I even find someone with a mental illness so attractive? Was he even a patient? Something about the sudden desire to flirt with this man made me a little uneasy. But the small tinge of uneasiness was dismayed by the utter curiosity boiling inside of me. In that moment I realized I had created my own version of what someone with mental illness looked like. It was in my best interest to learn all of the symptoms that would cause someone to be at their worst. I had spent my entire college career preparing myself to deal with people when they were at their worst. I was almost ashamed of the reality that I had never considered them having a best.

The light was glistening off of his smile. I thought that little twinkle was only for the movies. I hadn't spent time looking at anyone lately, especially men. Why was I so captivated with this man, this man who I wasn't even sure wasn't completely outside of his own mind? "Snap out of it Ella," I said to myself right before I squealed. Suddenly there was a woman a little older than me right beside me. "Jesus!"

"Be careful with Lebannon, he's quite the charmer," she said snickering. "Sorry I startled you, I figured you might have gotten lost. Mandy can be pretty vague with the directions," she lowered her tone to a whisper, "I'm not even sure why they keep her around, everyone complains about her terrible attitude."

I was a little confused, and this woman was talking so fast. I heard everything she said but couldn't help admiring the royal purple lipstick she was wearing. It was the perfect complexion for her olive skin. Her voice was a little high pitched but was warm and welcoming. It had a southern draw to it that reminded me of home. She made me want to call my mom as soon as I left.

"So sorry hun, I'm justa rambling away. I'm Candy, one of the nurses here at the Asylum, nice to meet you." She raised her hand to shake. Her nails were perfectly polished and just the right length.

"Ella. Candy's a pretty name."

"Oh, hunny no need to try and make me feel good. I know it sounds like my mom expected me to be a stripper or something. Trust me, I heard it all in school. Ironically, my mom just craved candy so much when she was pregnant with me that's where I got my name. She was right lazy with it if you ask me," she chuckled at herself.

I motioned behind me through the large glass window, "So, Lebannon?" My tone came out more inquisitively playful than I expected it to.

"Yeah, he's one of the most dapper patients we have by far. Like I said, he's quite the charmer, and a big flirt, so be careful. Come on with me, I'll give you the grand tour." She swiftly twisted around on her heels and started walking. "This is what we call the Rec Room. All of our patients have free time for the majority of the day as long as they are not on lockdown. Some of them like to use the Rec Room to watch TV, play cards, pretty much anything they want to that won't harm them. Others like to spend their time in their rooms. It all really just depends on the day around here."

"Lockdown?" I asked trying to keep up.

"Yes, sometimes the patients may have episodes and become a danger to themselves mostly, but sometimes to others, so they may have

ONE

to be heavily medicated and on a lockdown procedure, which we will go over shortly. On the opposite side of this hallway are different offices. Most of them are labeled like the linen closet, as well as a few of the therapists' offices. The ones that don't have labels on them are only used for storage."

The hallway and Rec Room seemed to go on forever. It was way larger than I could have imagined, but that made since. The asylum was huge itself. I tried to make mental note of everything I saw, getting lost in a place this big wasn't what I wanted to do. Finally we came to the end of the hallway.

"To the right leads you to the hospital ward as well as the morgue. Unfortunately, sometimes we use that place a little more often than we would like. We don't have a dedicated coroner so sometimes it can take up to a week to get one here to autopsy patients and fully document for the families. If they have families. Interestingly enough, for those who don't have families or anyone who claims their bodies, we also have our own cemetery at the far end at the back of the property."

"Wow, really?" I had never heard of that before. So far, listening to Candy was making this internship even more interesting. I just didn't know how interesting it would continue to get as the day progressed.

"Yeah, it's pretty interesting. To the left here we have a few more offices, the cafeteria where you'll be able to get lunch or snacks during your break, and there's also a faculty breakroom. Let's head back towards the other offices to have you fill out your NDA and other HR documents."

"An NDA?" My sudden confusion had halted my pace. I didn't even realize I stopped walking when I asked the question.

"Yes, no one told you? Oh goodness you have to do everything yourself if you want it done right these days. Given the patients here are all in very vulnerable states and can be seen at their worst, you have to agree not to disclose what happens here with patients to people not employed by the clinic."

"I don't mean to sound rude Candy, but if I can't disclose things, how am I to properly complete my assignments for the internship course?"

"The only exception is to your professor. The school's Psych department has a standing NDA with Henry Ellin. Your assignments just shouldn't be shared or proofed with other students.

"Wow," that's all I could say. The rest of the brief walk was quiet. It was honestly the first time Candy had stopped talking since she introduced herself. We passed back by the Rec Room window. Lebannon was still sitting in the corner, seemingly playing cards with himself. Almost as if he knew I was staring at him as I walked by, he looked up again. There was a slight smile on his face. It was as if he knew he had grabbed my attention. And he had.

TWO

We finally made it to an office that was filled with clutter and had a dingy feel to it. I couldn't help but think that place needed serious renovation. The building had to have been over two hundred years old, and it showed throughout each room.

"Here's the NDA, and other paperwork. Read through it and sign your name at the bottom. I'll be right down the hall," Candy said, hurrying out of the dingy yellow room as if she were late for something. The stack of papers in front of me was daunting. I always hated reading through paperwork, but I couldn't imagine signing something that I didn't fully understand. I took a deep breath, let out a big sigh and started reading.

At the top of the list was typical HR information. My contact information, emergency contacts, etc. There was a release of liability to ensure I wouldn't sue the asylum in the event something happened to me while there. After about ten minutes of reading and signing, I finally found myself on the last page of the packet. I couldn't help but think this could have all been emailed prior to my first day, but oh well.

The NDA was the last page I needed to sign. It seemed pretty straightforward for the most part, but it did have some odd verbiage. There were statements like, "Agreement to refrain from disclosing patient diagnosis and/or sentence." The use of the word sentence there was a little confusing, what did they mean sentence? Were there criminals that were housed here? There was also a line that said, "Agreement to refrain from disclosing client name, whereabouts, and/or overall wellbeing." Why would that even be necessary?

I hadn't signed many NDA's in my day, and despite a few lines raising my eyebrow a little, I needed to sign to ensure I could get my internship finished on time. I had procrastinated for the last two semesters and couldn't put it off anymore; I needed to finish this to graduate. I quickly signed my name and stuffed the papers in the manila envelope Candy left for me. I scribbled my name and the date on the envelope and headed out to find her.

I walked up and down the same hall for a few minutes looking for Candy to no avail. Just as I was about to turn the corner Candy and a number of nurses and orderlies ran past me. "We've got a runner!" I heard someone yell in the commotion. I wasn't sure what I should do. I wasn't even sure what they were doing. Was someone trying to escape?

I swiftly walked towards where the others had run. Rounding the corner, I could see about four male nurses, or orderlies, wrestling with a patient. "I can't be around him! He's going to kill me! Please, help me!" The patient was screaming to the top of his lungs. I could see him frantically trying to get away from them. He seemed desperate. I had never seen anything like it. Candy stood there with a needle with what no doubt had to contain some type of concoction of medication that would sedate him. Another woman stood there holding a straight jacket, patiently waiting for one of the men to grab it.

"Jacory, we've been over this. No one is out to get you hunny, just calm down." Candy said warmly with her southern drawl.

"I don't want to die; he's trying to kill me. Why aren't you listening?!" Jacory screamed back, still putting up a good fight with the men. He was pretty strong for someone his size. He couldn't have been any taller than I was, maybe about five nine. He wasn't a large statured man. Honestly, he was quite skinny. I couldn't make out how old he was, but his hair was starting to gray in the front and I could vaguely make out a few wrinkles starting to form on his face. Given the state I was seeing

TWO

him in though, I wasn't too sure of all of his features. A portion of his body and his face was blocked by one of the orderlies.

"Ella, hunny," Candy called, jumping back as she passed the ruckus to come towards me. She was very small and petite, but you could tell she ran the place. Watching her jump and miss all of the large muscular men made me think she was an Olympian in a past life. "Whew, the chases always have me out of breath, you'd think I'd be in shape working in such a large building," she said chuckling, as if what was happening right behind her was no big deal. My eyes must have been wide open, staring, because she reached out and rubbed my arm saying, "Oh sug, this isn't anything to be worried about. Jacory has just gone and gotten himself a little paranoid is all." She lowered her tone to a whisper, "As you can see, he seems to think someone is out to kill him. We go through this once a week or so with him. He tries to escape, we have to sedate him and enforce lockdown procedures with. Once his lockdown is over, and we do it all again. Fun times really, he's probably the most consistent man in my life."

If I wasn't so confused, and amazed, at the situation at hand I would have howled laughing. I was starting to realize Candy was quite quick on her feet with the jokes. "Well, who does he think is trying to kill him?" My tone came out more alarmed than I had expected it to.

Candy looked at me with her sweet, warm eyes. In the calmest tone I have ever heard she said, "Sweetheart, a part of Jacory's condition makes him paranoid. He always thinks a fellow patient is trying to kill him. There's nothing to be concerned about, other than insuring we get Jacory the proper medication and back to his room to rest."

I heard what she was saying, but for some reason I wasn't convinced. I'm not sure if it was the desperation in his voice, or in his constant battle because of it, but there seemed to be a genuine fear inside of this man. Not one that was encouraged by paranoia. Candy was still rambling away about procedures and what would happen next, but I was fixated on Jacory. At this point there were tears streaming down his deep brown face. His hair was unkept. I was going to have to ask if they bothered to have any barbers around this place for patients. His beard was just the same, not making his situation better. I thought I saw a flash of scars underneath his beard but couldn't quite make out anything. Everything was happening so quickly. He looked like a homeless man on the streets throwing a tantrum. But inside of his eyes, there was a fear like no other. Something had really happened to this man. There was something in this place that was causing him to behave this way, and it wasn't just his condition. If he was on the proper medication his paranoid episodes would be minimal, not a weekly occurrence.

I figured it was too early to share my feelings with Candy, I mean who was I anyway? It was my first day, and I was simply a college intern. Who would listen to my opinion and take it seriously around here? She had already seemed to write off what he had been experiencing.

I was taken out of my own thoughts just in time to hear Candy say, "Why don't you head down to the Rec Room and observe some of the patients in there. Lowering her voice again she said, "If you're lucky, maybe there won't be many, and you can have the TV all to yourself." Giggling she hurried back towards Jacory and the others. She yelled back over her shoulder, throwing up her hand, "I'll be up to get you as soon as we're done here."

I turned back toward the direction I came. "Doesn't she know I have no idea where anything is around here?" I quietly asked myself. As soon as the words left my mouth, I realized it would probably be best that I not make it a point to talk to myself while in the asylum. At least not visibly. Didn't want to give off the wrong impression too soon. Wouldn't want to end up with a group of muscle ridden men surrounding me wanting to put me in a straight jacket while a petite little southern lady stuck me with a needle. That seemed like something out of a movie, yet that's where I had found myself. I had to admit; this internship assignment was proving to be quite eventful. Definitely nothing at all like what I expected.

TWO

I checked my watch, 9:30. I had gotten there at about 7:45. It didn't seem like that much time had already passed. I was supposed to leave around five that afternoon. If the rest of the day went anything like the last hour and a half, I knew it would fly by. I couldn't wait to get back to my apartment to start working on my first assignment. I was to write a three-page essay on what my first day as an intern was like, to include what I observed, and what my thoughts were on how patients were being diagnosed.

At first, I thought that assignment sounded elementary in nature. Who was I to have an opinion one way or another on how an established institution dealt with and diagnosed their patients? After this morning though, I was sure I would have plenty to write about. Suddenly I felt overwhelmed at the notion that what I wrote could cause an investigation into the Asylum's practices. I quickly waved that thought away. I was being unrealistic. *Was this place getting to me already?*

Before I knew it, I looked up and found myself standing in front of the wall length window looking into the Rec Room.

Lebannon was still sitting in the same spot, staring back at me.

THREE

Had I not been immediately intrigued; I would have found it rather creepy that this man was staring at me when I looked up. I had stopped walking and was just standing in the middle of the hallway, looking into this man's eyes from the opposite side of the glass. They were so deep and intoxicating. I wasn't really looking into him though, moreso his eyes seemingly made me look into myself. It was like staring down a long dark hallway, with just a tiny speck of light at the end. Something about that speck made me feel good. It made me want to get closer.

His eyes were completely different than what I had seen with Jacory. In Jacory's eyes was nothing but fear and desperation. In Lebannon's eyes, however, there was something light and welcoming. At that point I obviously knew he was a patient, but I couldn't help but think if I had run into him on the streets, I wouldn't have ever imagined he struggled with his mental health. For a moment, that made me feel defeated. I was studying to be able to diagnose people like this and I was quickly realizing that there were some I wouldn't be able to pick out of a crowd. I pushed that thought to the side by focusing on the fact that one day I would be skilled enough to be able to treat someone so well that no one else knew they had a diagnosis. Not even other professionals.

I figured Candy would be a little while, so I pushed open the large steal doors leading into the Rec Room. There. I was on the other side of the glass window. It smelled fresh, much fresher than the hallway or the little room I filled out my paperwork in. It was almost a sterile clean smell, but more appealing than a hospital operating room. Hints of lavender and laods of lemon quickly filled my nostrils, reminding me of a crisp spring afternoon.

I walked around for a moment, pretending not to notice Lebannon following me with his eyes. The woman by the TV was gone, but the young man had since taken her spot. Now that the glass window wasn't in between us, I could see he was indeed drooling. I stood there for a moment, watching the soft rise and fall of his chest with each breath. He was so still I couldn't imagine him having moved from his previous spot to this one.

I walked a little closer to him, putting a smile on my face. "Hey there, I'm Ella."

"I hate to break it to ya Ella, but ole Ron there won't talk back. Can't really." It was Lebannon. We were the only other ones in the Rec Room, so his voice carried without him having to raise it. He reminded me of home too. His voice had a twang to it that Candy's didn't have though. His words were drawn out a little more than hers, but not in a way that I couldn't understand him. I wasn't sure if he enunciated and articulated very well, or if I could just hear him clearly because I was southern myself. Either way, his accent intrigued me all the more. I always have been a sucker for a twangy accent.

I wanted to know more about him. In some ways, I think I wanted to see if I could pinpoint his diagnosis myself.

I turned and walked toward his corner of the room. "Lebannon, your reputation precedes you. Now can Ron really not speak, or were you just trying to snatch my attention away from him?" It came out flirtier than I intended. What was happening to me? There was no turning back now; I had to see what was so engulfing about this particular patient. My heart rate picked up, beating a few more paces a second than it had been earlier. Was it the anxiety associated with being in a new situation? Or was it Lebannon and I's interaction?

THREE

Quickly I tossed the latter thought out of my mind. Why would my heart rate increase just by talking to this man? I certainly couldn't find myself attracted to him, could I? No of course not, that was definitely against some sort of ethical code. I went with being in a new situation. That was the safest explanation for my increased heart rate.

"Well Miss Ella, Ron there is a borderline vegetable. They keep him dosed up pretty good around here so he don't do much talking."

A vegetable was an interesting way to describe someone who wasn't a coma patient. "If he's such a "vegetable," how did he move from where he was earlier?"

"Every now and again he gets up and goes for a little walk," he couldn't hold in his laughter. "I'm just messin', I like to see the look on you newcomers face when you think the vegetable moved on his own. I move him around from time to time in here. I'm sure he gets bored with the same view. You play?" He held up the deck of cards he had been shuffling.

His skin was almost perfect. He was probably a deep olive complexion in his younger days. It had long since lost it's vibrance, I figured he'd probably been in the asylum for a while. I could only imagine that natural sunlight was lacking for the patients. He had become a much paler complexion of what he once was. I could tell he wasn't naturally this light. His head was shaved bald, but his long stringy beard was sandy brown, speckled with grey hairs. There were small wrinkles starting to form in the crevices of his face, but you wouldn't know until you were looking closely.

"Depends on what you're playing." I responded.

"21? That's a pretty simple one."

"Blackjack? Yes, I can play that." I was vaguely familiar with the term 21 but had always called in blackjack. He smiled and started shuffling the cards. That's when I noticed the scars on his hands.

FOUR

I wonder if they're rough. That's all I could think as we played a few hands. The scars on his hand became much more noticeable as I looked closer. The skin there looked as if it had been torn and sewn back in place. To the naked eye, it looked textured. Some areas of his hand seemed lifted while others seemed to smoothly run across his hand.

They were more like burns than scars, or maybe scars from a skin graft. I wasn't sure exactly, but I could tell they went a ways up his arms. He was wearing a thick, long sleeved button up; the kind you may see a maintenance man in. They made him all the more mysterious. Now, I not only wanted to try to figure out his diagnosis and what got him there, but also what happened to his arms.

I pulled myself away from my thoughts long enough to realize at least thirty minutes must have passed by.

"If you're waiting for Candy, she'll be a minute. Jacory can be quite the character when he is in full blown episode." How did he know I was wondering where Candy was? I convinced myself it probably wasn't that hard to put together. Candy seemed to be the one in charge around here, and I was sitting there playing cards with a patient obviously waiting for something. I was starting to get too deep into my own head though. I couldn't help but find it strange that Lebannon took advantage of the first opportunity he could to talk to me, but now I was right in front of him and he wasn't saying as much as I expected him to.

Who was I kidding; this was a patient in an asylum, why was I thinking things that should only concern me on a date? I wasn't on a date. But then again, this was a new experience. It was so intriguing for me and I had no idea how to really feel. From what was so mysterious about this man to what was happening inside my own mind. This first day had turned from a disappointing assignment into a psychological puzzle, and I was enjoying the game.

"Jacory has those episodes often?" I asked, gently picking up the cards he had just dealt me.

"Seems to be about once a week these days. It wasn't so bad when he first got here, but for some reason the poor fella is just convinced there's someone in here out to get him. It kind of came out of the blue one day. He's had regularly occurring episodes ever since."

"You were here when he first got here?" It seemed like the perfect opportunity to try to pry information from him. I couldn't resist throwing that in there. I was eagerly awaiting his response, fidgeting with the cars in my hands. Looking at them, at the deck, and back at the cards again. Replaying that back doesn't sound smooth at all though.

"Yes ma'am," his country twang reminded me of a southern gentleman holding the door open for a lady at the grocery with cowboy boots and jeans on. "I been here about, oh, what year is it?"

I wasn't sure if he was joking or serious, but I stared in shock.

"I'm just messin' darling," he chuckled. "I been in here about eight years now."

The ball was rolling. Eight years. That seemed like a pretty long time for someone to be in an asylum and still be so, normal? I couldn't help but admit to myself that I had done something I thought I would never do as a major in this field. I had completely created the wrong narrative of what people with mental illness look like. From them having good days, to what I expected the inside of this asylum to be like. I had prepared myself to deal with more of the Jacory's and the Ron's. Lebannon was on a completely different level. A level I hadn't considered, and must admit I hadn't even learned about. While I was completely enthralled with finding out all I could about him, I couldn't help but wonder how many others where within the asylum walls who wouldn't fit the bill of what I expected them to look and behave like.

"I know, I don't look like I've been in the nut house for eight years huh?"

"It's not a nut house."

"Sure. Listen hun, a lot of us in here ain't stupid. We know you "professionals" like to make us feel good and such, but we also know what other folk out there in the real world call a fine establishment such as this one." His twang and sarcasm caused the word professionals to be drawn out longer than any other word, but I understood his point. He was right. We had been taught over and over again to try to help the community destigmatize mental illness and restructure the way we use words. The reality was that was a stigma well before I got in college, and everyone knew it.

I had just won the hand we were playing when he suddenly leaned over, interrupting the small, ridiculous celebration in my head at my victory. "Wanna know the secret?" He was whispering. His body language reminded me of the woman who was talking to herself earlier. Just thinking about her made me even more conscious about how long I had been sitting there. Candy still hadn't shown back up.

I leaned in forward, looking over toward Ron. For some reason I felt I needed to play the part too. I found myself becoming a character to get information, rather than an aspiring psychiatrist attempting a diagnosis. Was I being bamboozled?

I nodded.

He looked around cautiously. It was the first time he seemed really serious about something. I got the feeling that he had been waiting to tell someone whatever he was about to say for a while.

"I don't take all the medicine they try to pump me with," his whisper was harsh, and his accent made it a little difficult to be sure I heard him correctly.

"You don't take your medicine?"

"Shhhhhh!" His hands flailed for a moment as if he wanted to cover my mouth. "Don't be so loud!"

I was startled. I wasn't expecting his movement to be so quick and aggressive, but I played along anyway. Lowering my voice this time, I tried to explain with reason, "The medication regimen your psychiatrist puts you on is designed to help you. Why wouldn't you take it? You see how Jacory acts."

His well-structured face was serious. I could see his jaws clenched down and his fists were squeezed tightly together. He saw me again glancing at his hands.

"These are the reasons why I don't and can't."

I was confused. "What do you mean?"

"Medication works for those who have something wrong with them. For those who don't have anything wrong with them, it turns them into someone else. I got tired of my mind being a puddle of mush, somewhat like ole Ron over there. You see, these scars on my arms and hands," he pulled up his sleeves just enough to show me the scars traced from his hands, up his wrists and forearms. Just as I suspected. "I got these from my position at my old job. They are the reason I'm here."

I was completely lost. His job was the reason he was in the asylum? His job caused the scars? Or was he saying because of the scars he had to become a patient here? Either way, I couldn't believe this man was admitting to me that he wasn't taking his medication. I wasn't quite sure what I had gotten myself into at that point. Something in the back of my mind stood up on high alert. A patient who hasn't been taking his meds? That couldn't be good. But there was still something about him so calm and charming, not at all like the paranoid demeanor of Jacory earlier.

FOUR

My curiosity abandoned my reason. I should have excused myself to find Candy. I should have alerted staff that he wasn't taking his medication. But could I believe what he was saying? I still didn't even know his diagnosis. I was too curious about his scars and his previous eight years here that I sat there. I wanted to get up, but I couldn't.

Instead, I looked at him. There was a little desperation in his worn eyes. But not the same kind of fear led desperation I saw in Jacory. This was the desperation to be heard. To tell someone a secret. "What do you mean those are why you are here? Your scars? How did they get you here?"

He leaned back in his chair. Things had gotten so intense that I barely realized he was only inches from my face, his body leaning halfway across the table. He looked around again, to make sure no one had come into the room. He no longer spoke in a hushed, whispered tone, but he was still mindful of how loud he allowed himself to speak.

"My job is the reason I have these scars. More so my position at the job. But they are the reason I am in here. They put me here to keep me quiet about what they were doing."

There was something inside of me that clicked. It was as if a switch inside of me went from the professional side of the switch over to conspiracy theorist. I spent my free time looking into conspiracy theories and mysteries. Unsolved cases were my favorite. You would think I took up something in the criminal justice department, but that was just something I did to occupy my mind. I had never been put in a position to choose between my deep desire for a good conspiracy or mystery and my love for psychology before. I felt like I was the school was testing me somehow and so far, I was failing miserably. It didn't seem to matter in the moment though. I was completely invested. I had to control the desire creeping up inside of me to blurt out as many questions as he could answer. He didn't seem like the kind of guy who I should question, so I had to roll with the punches.

"What kind of job would do that?" I asked instinctually. It came out rather harsh. It wasn't like me to question someone's competence, evern if they were in a mental institution. Though there was a desire to know more burning a hole inside of me, I hadn't completely lost reason and reality. At least not yet.

"Nobody would believe me if I told them what happened anyway. I don't even know why this was necessary. But just the thought that someone would actually believe me, well I guess that was enough to land me here," trailing off, he looked off to the side. I hadn't noticed before but right behind him was a small window overlooking the parking lot. There was a large circular driveway going up to the front of the asylum. It circled a large grassy area with a statue in the middle. I didn't recognize the man the statue was made after, the founder no doubt. It was old and worn, but it seemed to get more attention and upkeep than the inside of the building itself. Just past the statue, on the other side of the lot I could see my raggedy old car.

I didn't say anything for a while. I didn't know what to say really. Besides that, though, I watched his behavior. His body language had calmed from the tense state it was in when he first mentioned not taking his medication. He wasn't fidgeting or shuffling around in his chair. He just sat there for a moment, blankly staring out the small window. He was recalling something. His eyelids fluttered back and forth, as if they were trying to keep up with the reel of pictures only he could see. My thoughts were louder than anything else in the room.

"Were you a welder?" I asked after a while, tired of the silence. Once I gathered my own thoughts and placed them in their respective corners of my mind, they weren't so loud anymore. It had gotten so quiet I thought I could hear the drool dripping from Ron's mouth hitting the floor.

His chuckle startled me. It seemed to fill the room, but it was soft at the same time. That question really tickled him. He seemed to laugh forever. It went from a small chuckle to a full-blown laugh attack. The

FOUR

infectious kind. Before I knew it, I was laughing and had no idea what was so funny. Our banter floated around the room, bouncing off the white sterile walls back at us.

"What are we laughing at?" I managed after a while.

"The irony of the question," he said, breaking after each word.

"Irony?"

Finally, we both calmed down enough for him to explain.

"Yes Ella, the irony. Had I been a regular ole welder, I probably wouldn't be sitting here talking to you."

"You don't think so?"

"I know so. My job was a bit more… complicated."

"Complicated?"

"Yes," he picked up the deck of cards and started shuffling. "I worked for a company, BLKQ. I worked in the local headquarters. I really didn't know how big this place was when I started, it just kind of fell into my lap. I learned later that wasn't the case at all. It's kind of funny actually, I was just like you when I was hired on."

"Just like me?"

"Yes'm. You see I started there as an intern. I was getting my Master's in Psychology."

"You have a MAS?" The words flowed out of my mouth quicker than I could adjust the shock that accompanied them on the way out.

"Yes Ella," his chuckling let me know he wasn't offended by my shocked response. "Believe it or not I'm not a nut, and I had a life before it was halted 8 years ago."

"I didn't mean it like that."

He laughed again, this time it seemed a little less genuine. "I'm sure. But yes, I was an intern at this large corporation. It was the worst thing that ever happened to me."

FIVE

According to my watch it had been an hour and a half since Candy sent me down to the Rec Room. I was starting to think she forgot about me. I couldn't help but wonder, briefly, if Lebannon wasn't in this room what I'd have been doing with all that time. It was just a brief flash of a thought though. My brain had started to run rampant since Lebannon said interning at that company was the worst thing that ever happened to him. This internship so far had been nothing like I expected, could this have been a bad decision? Should I have tried harder to find a different internship, one more like what I wanted to do? Why was I over exaggerating?

My thoughts started to betray me. I ran through tens of scenarios and reasons why this internship could have been a terrible mistake. All absolutely absurd if brought to the light of reality. But it didn't matter, my mind ran it's way. I tried to slow it down by thinking of all the reasons why interning could have ended so terribly for Lebannon. In all the scenarios I pictured for the both of us, they were all disgustingly far from the reality.

"Did you not enjoy the job?" It was the first time either of us had spoken in a while. We had played about three more games of Blackjack before I knew what to say. There was only the sound of shuffling cards and the occasional "hit me."

"Oh, I loved the job, when I was an intern." He was hesitant to continue. Sighing he went on, "My internship was for two months. At the end of the two months, I knew there was a possibility that a permanent position could be offered based on how the company felt about my performance at graduation. Like I said, the internship was great." He startled shuffling again, "You want to play something different?"

"Up to you," I said.

He shuffled the cards for a while before choosing to just look through them. One by one he flipped over a card, revealing the numbers and symbols underneath before putting it into the new pile he had created.

"I remember my first day like it was yesterday. I can bet it was way better than yours is today too," he smiled, looking up at me. There was a slight twinkle in his eyes, the same twinkle I had seen through the glass window earlier. "I was so excited. The opportunity was more amazing than I could have ever imagined. It wasn't even an internship that I had applied for, but my professor did. He said he thought I would be great for the program they had. The potential for a job offer alone was enough. At that point in my college career, I was extremely worried about how I was going to pay back all the money I borrowed for school. The potential offer after the internship was more than enough to cover those costs and ensure I was able to live comfortably. It was the kind of salary that I could have only imagined throughout school."

He started a new deck to continue flipping the cards over and out of the deck in his hand. I noticed he started to separate black and red cards.

"I pulled up the first day nervous as all get out, but I was determined. I wanted to make a lasting impression. I wanted more than the experience; I wanted that position in two months. It was going to be life changing for me.

I went to a thrift shop a few days before to get a new shirt and tie. I wasn't completely broke, but I knew I couldn't spend the kind of money people in that place spent on suits. So, I looked high and low and found the perfect outfit. It was perfect to me at least. The light yellow button up seemed to call my name. It was vibrant, but calm at the same time. Not too terribly flashy. It caught my eye, tucked behind a pile of other

FIVE

shirts with designs and patterns. It peaked out from behind a silk colorblock button up, just enough to call my eyes over to bring it to the light. Perfect. I already had a nice pair of khaki slacks. The only thing I needed was a tie. As if on que, a tie drew my attention, much like the yellow shirt did. It was white with blue stripes and yellow polka dots. Oh, I was excited.

When I first walked in it was calm. The calm before the storm. A nice woman, Chelsty greeted me. She was all business, but oh so beautiful. She was just a little shorter than me, but her heels put her about an inch above my head. Her hair was sleeked back into a high ponytail. It was bone straight and the ponytail went down her back. She had a clipboard in hand and walked faster than I expected. I was so nervous, and awe struck with how amazing she looked I fumbled trying to keep up with her.

The front entrance was grand and there was a large receptionist desk that sat in the middle. There were two corridors directly behind the receptionist. Above the doorway to the left it said, "Client Relations" while the doorway towards the right said, "Employees Only." Chelsty led us through the right entrance. The ceiling in the hall was extraordinary. Soon we entered a room so magnificent I would have never guessed it to be there.

There were offices lining one wall; some with windows to see inside, others were just doors with smaller windows on them. There was a cluster of cubicle like desks to one side. Another large desk was directly beside the entrance, where a young lady, whose name tag read Claire greeted us.

'Good Morning Chelsty, is this the new intern?' Oh, her smile was radiant. She was beautiful. Her skin was a much deeper complexion than Chelsty's, almost as if all of the colors of the rainbow melted together and created her. I could tell her skin was soft, polished. I wasn't sure if she had makeup on, but it didn't matter. Her eyes were large and round.

Captivating really. She smelled sweet, like a combination of sugar and flowers. It was intoxicating."

Lebannon's demeanor shifted. The more he talked about Claire, the more I realized she must have been very important to him. "Did you ask her out?" I interrupted him, mid sentence.

He stared at me blankly for a moment, I wasn't sure if he was recalling that moment or stunned that I cut him off so bluntly. Finally, he blinked his eyes a few times and smirked.

"Well, if you don't cut me off, you'll get the whole story now won't ya," he smiled and carried on. "I was stuck somewhere between not trying to stare at her and staring at her for one too many seconds. I stumbled a little bit, embarrassing myself in front of her like a schoolboy. It didn't seem to phase her though, maybe annoyed Chelsty a little, but that's about it. She actually smiled at me and said, 'It's okay, everyone is nervous on their first day here. Hell depending on the day, everyone may be nervous here.'

I smiled back at her, thanking her for the reassurance. In the back of my mind though, I did wonder what she meant about everyone being nervous. I had tried to do research on what it was like to work for the company before my first day, but interestingly enough there were no reviews anywhere. I couldn't find anything from an employee's perspective. I learned quickly why."

"21!" My sudden outburst made him jump. It was subtle enough, but I could see and slightly hear the scuffing of his chair against the floor as he twitched a little startled.

"Don't get too excited, I let you win that time." He tried to play it off. I let him. I couldn't understand how his teeth were so perfect when he had been in here for so long. Making a mental note to ask Candy if they staffed Dentist's and other medical professionals to keep the patients up, I nodded for him to continue. "I remember Claire interrupting Chelsty, who had been talking for a while. She was probably explaining things about the job and business, but I was too star struck with Claire to take conscious note.

Mr. Linguh was ready for us. Chelsty quickly started walking again, asking that I follow her. I fumbled away with her, looking back to give Claire one last smile, hopefully not making a complete idiot of myself.

The stairs seemed to go on forever. Seeing the staircase from across the first floor didn't do them justice now that I was walking up them. There was detailing on the rail, and the stairs themselves were marble but slightly textured. I wasn't sure if the texture helped keep my dress shoes from slipping beneath me, or if it slightly made it worse. One thing I did know, trying to ensure I kept my balance on that stairway was taking everything in me. I remember wondering if Chelsty was actually trotting up those stairs as effortlessly as she seemed to be, or if on the inside her entire body was tense and engaged like mine. I felt like I had done a hundred sit ups, and all I was doing was walking up the stairs.

By the time we reached the top of the staircase I found myself out of breath. I wasn't a gym rat or anything like that, but I felt like I was in decent shape. Those stairs either proved me wrong or proved I had gained a few college pounds. Either way, I was trying hard not to dramatically gasp for air. Chelsty was still hurriedly walking ahead of me too, so I had to keep up.

She must have realized my thoughts on why we had to basically run around the building, so she offered an explanation, 'Mr. Linguh isn't the most patient man. He's going to be your direct supervisor, unfortunately. Luckily for you though, he has a little more respect for men than women, but not by much. If he takes to you, and actually likes you, run with it and don't do anything to make him question it. I've looked at your resume, and I believe as long as you don't make a complete fool of yourself, you can start out pretty high on his scale. Smile, nod, and agree with what he says. Laugh at his jokes and engage in the conversation, but not so much that he thinks you're trying to steal the limelight. You think you can handle that?'

I said yes as I nodded, but my stomach said otherwise. It was as if my stomach was turning over on itself and my intestines were quickly suffocating themselves. Knots were forming, and my anxiety was already creating doubts and frustrations at the thought of meeting this man. But I had to stay focused. If I could get on his good side the first day, and stay there for two months, I was bound to ensure I was offered the full-time contract once my internship was over. I was also starting to recall Chelsty's rambling on when we were with Claire, something along the lines of full-time employees having their student loans completely paid for by the company. Keeping that in the back of my mind, I made sure to be as impressive as possible."

The silence after his last sentence was deafening. For a brief moment everything in the room was intensified. I could hear the air flowing from the vents, a loud gushing noise as the air conditioner exploded on. The sudden swish as Lebannon shuffled the deck of cards. I looked around for the ticking time piece that suddenly invaded my ear drums, but I found none. It must have been an old analog in the hallway. All the sounds combined seemed to put me in a trance with my own thoughts.

I was patiently waiting for him to continue his conversation. Meanwhile my thoughts started to swarm. I was faced with every doubt I had about myself, and my professionalism. I suddenly couldn't stop staring at his lips. They were perfectly moisturized, leaving just the faintest shine. My eyes were fixated on this lips,eagerly waiting for them to part as his breath escaped with words explaining what it was like in front of Mr. Linguh. *Why did I find myself yearning for more of whatever it was that he had to say, rather than being concerned about why Candy hadn't come for me yet?* I hoped he didn't notice me staring and get the wrong idea.

I couldn't bare it any longer, so I pierced through the silence. "What was it like meeting Mr. Linguh?"

FIVE

It seemed to startle him. He was much more jumpy than I would have expected him to be with his smooth demeanor. Suddenly I realized I had jolted him out of a daze with my question. Whatever place of remembrance he had gone to had completely taken him from where we were to another place. I wondered how long it had taken him to develop that skill in the asylum. Or maybe he had the skill before he was placed there.

Finally, he spoke. It had been quiet for what felt like years, making me forget the sultry voice that was his as it sliced through the room. "Chelsty was right about Mr. Linguh. He was more inclined to me because I was a male. He wasn't quite what I pictured him to be, I'll tell ya that. With a name like Linguh I almost expected him to be of Asian decent, but I was completely mistaken. I also, for some reason, envisioned him as a short, angry man. He was not that. Instead, I was led into a room with a tall, dark skinned man with a glistening bald head. His suit was tailored well to fit his athletic frame. His smile spread across his face from ear to ear. In that moment, I couldn't understand why Chelsty suggested that this was a stern, unlikable guy. His smile was wide and welcoming, he was handsome, and he greeted me as if we were old friends. I remember the sudden movement of his body as he seemed to jump towards me with his hand extended for a handshake.

He dismissed Chelsty, though it didn't seem disrespectful. He explained my job to me, gave me a tour of the facility, and everything was fine. There was always a part of the facility that I was never introduced to though, one that was seemingly off limits. I noticed one end of the hallway had a door. I could barely make out what looked to be a badge reader of some sort beside it. I hadn't seen any other doors with that type of mechanisms attached to it. It seemed somewhat out of place. I wanted the job, so I kept my pressing curiosity to myself. Maybe I shouldn't have."

SIX

"I don't think I really understand how a job, a prestigious job it sounds like, could have landed you in an..." My voice lowered unconsciously, "insane asylum."

My statement seemed to amuse Lebannon. It started with a small smirk. Before I knew it, his smirk turned to yet another infectious laugh, pulsating through the room. He had a way of doing that. I was chuckling but only because of the infectious laughter coming from deep down in his soul. I didn't understand what was so funny though, "Why is this so hilarious?" I managed.

"Ella," he finally said as his laughter subsided. It still took him a moment to get my name out on the first try without breaking out into a bout of laughter in the midst. "Ella," he started again. "The job I did during my two months as an intern was no where close to the job I was hired to do once I graduated."

The look on my face must have been one of pure confusion.

"You see, the job I did as an intern was more...administrative in nature. I saw a few employees a week to help them with the stress of the job. If I can be quite frank about this, I can't recall if I actually knew what the job description employees of this job was. I really had no idea what they did. Either way, I sat for weeks as an internal therapist. Young men and women came and left frequently, sometimes I even saw the same individuals. The stress levels in that building began to cause my office to sweat. At least that's how it felt to me. The room wreaked of people's tensions and problems. But, all in all, it was a decent gig. It wasn't really stressful for me, more so redundant.

Every so often, I found there were a few employees that were missin'."

"Messin'?" I interrupted; the country twang of his accent did make a few words difficult to understand, especially when they sounded so much like other words he used. I wanted to make sure I heard him correctly.

"No. Missin', like they weren't there anymore." I nodded. "I assumed people were fired or quit. The job seemed to have a high turn over rate. At least I figured it would based on the types of things folks came into my office to vent about. Either way, it wasn't that bad for me really. I sat there and listened to employee after employee, wondering why they chose to stay if they were so miserable. Honestly though, I was kind of excited."

"Excited?" My confusion came across thick, I only imagined what my facial expression said.

"Yes. Excited. With the amount of stress occurring in such a large place, they couldn't afford not to have a therapist or two. Knowing this, I made sure I never allowed the stress of my last patient to seep into a session with the next. I thought if I ensured that in the event they were asked how their therapy appointments went, they had nothing but good things to say about me. It was all a play at increasing my odds of being offered the permanent position really. It's amazing how much financial stress can shift the perspective of why you do what you do.

At the end of the day, my job wasn't the stressful one. All I had to do was listen to people complain about their jobs. It wasn't difficult for me at all. I was always going to get paid, and the company ensured there were strict time frames that were adhered to for counseling. This helped to ensure I wasn't overwhelmed. As far as a therapist goes, it was kind of easy."

"Easy?"

"Yes. Everyone had the same thing, and the treatment was pretty much the same across the board. There weren't a lot of differing diagnosis and I evaluated the same typical symptoms of stress. It was stuff

SIX

I had probably learned in year two. I don't know how eager you are to go around diagnosing people or trying to identify what symptoms are affecting what parts of their lives, but that wasn't me. Yeah, I absolutely wanted to be a therapist. There were multiple things I looked forward to doing once graduation came, but of the utmost importance was my financial stability. This was the cream of the crop as far as job opportunities went. The pay was going to be well over what I could have expected, with benefits. And all in all, it wasn't very stressful for me. Till it was of course."

"I don't know what school was like when you were studying, but surely you had to know just from your college experience that there was going to be a level of stress with any job out there." I found it odd that he didn't expect much stress from his job. Given that the only reason he, or someone of his education and skill, was needed was because of the stress level of the company. Even I knew listening to him that at some point that stress would infiltrate his own job description.

"I went to grad school. I was very familiar with stress. Not having it, even when everyone else around me seemed to be so affected by it was a rarity. I was grateful. But eventually, the job description itself changed. I faced something that I couldn't have ever imagined. Often times I wonder if I sold my soul to the devil."

There wasn't much else evident in our conversation to make me feel that this country twang speaking man was religious. I didn't know where he was going with this, but I was also curious to know what kind of job would be so bad. There seemed to be a dramatic shift in what he said he felt as an intern to what he experienced as a full-time employee. I couldn't help but think about myself. By no means would I be interested in seeking a full-time position in that asylum when the internship was over, but so far it was a piece of cake. I had been sitting there talking with the same patient while the person I was supposed to be shadowing did whatever. Seemed like an easy A to me.

Then again, I realized the motivations we had going into our internship experiences were completely different. I just needed to pass the class, check the box, and move on. I wasn't the wealthiest, and my family wasn't rich, but I wasn't as concerned about my financial stability after college as he seemed to have been.

Sitting there, in that sterile white room, with a handsome man who just so happened to also be a patient at a mental facility seemed to teach me so much about myself. I had experienced more emotions sitting there with Lebannon than I cared to share. First of all, I'm sure there were moments I was there, sitting across from him, flirtatiously clinging to the conversation. In my mind, what was wrong with being attracted to a man who may have a few issues. Though I also knew that had I said that out loud to any of my friends, they would follow it up with something like, "Everything!" "You don't even know what's wrong with him." Things that made it sound extremely ridiculous. Not to mention, it was definitely unethical. Or at least unprofessional at the bare minimum.

But it came so easy. The way talking to him made me feel was something out of a movie. My heart beat just a little faster when he spoke. My ears perked up whenever he used my name in conversation. It was harmless enough, but so wrong to feel at the same time. The kind of wrong and right you may feel dirty dancing with the devil. I had to keep my flirtations to a minimum, I knew that, but it was proving more difficult. A sweet voice, bantering eyes, and the occasional half smile all betrayed my every effort to keep things strictly as a professional curiosity.

That wasn't the only thing though. Hearing why maintaining that job was so important made me realize that I was much better off than others, even my friends. I got scholarships, and a small trust my parents had managed to keep for me specifically for college. Of course I wanted to make sure I obtained a good job after graduation, but I was afforded the unique position to be able to look for the job that was optimal for me. It wasn't about what paid the most money, though that was a factor.

SIX

"It doesn't make right sense to you does it?" His voice startled me. I had become enthralled with my thoughts and was so wrapped up in what I had been thinking and feeling, I almost forgot he was there.

"I don't quite understand the question," the words came out a bit harsher than I anticipated. I figured I knew what he was talking about; the same thing I was thinking about. Having it brought to my attention out loud didn't sit well with me in that moment.

"That reasoning don't make sense to you because it ain't something that heavily affects you. You aren't very wealthy, but you're well off enough to not have to have those types of concerns and thoughts that may put you in a situation like me. Am I right?"

I was taken aback with his observation, what was he a profiler or something? "Well, I don't know how to answer that question, considering I still have no clue what your situation really is." My suddenly sharp tone surprised me more than it seemed to affect him. I found myself offended, but he wasn't wrong. Maybe that's why I was so annoyed with what he was saying.

"Even if that's true, Ella, I can tell by the tone of frustration in your pretty little voice that you know I'm right. But since I am a gentleman, I'll say you're right as well there darlin'. I haven't even given you a glimpse into what things were really like. You still don't know what the situation was that landed me in a place where I listen to folks talk to themselves and watch others slobber all over the place."

At his pause I couldn't help but look over at Ron. He was right. I didn't know how he was right, but I just felt like he was. I knew he was completely different from the other patients I had been exposed to. They all seemed visibly distraught or more so like they belonged. He didn't. Because of that, I desperately wanted to know what had landed him here. There was a desire in me to figure out why he was so different from everyone else. It was quite burning.

"Yes, you're right," a little voice inside my head was screaming at me for admitting that out loud. "You are seemingly different than the other patients I've met so far. I'm curious to know the real reason as to why you're in here. So, what happened? And I haven't forgotten that I asked if you went out with Claire and I have yet to receive an answer."

"Well, I'm not finished with the story, am I hun?"

"You're mighty long winded, hun." I was proud of the snarky comment I had made with the use of his own pet names. He smirked, picking up the sarcasm as if it added flame to the back and forth we were playing. There was the small inkling of desire sitting at the pit of my stomach, toying with the idea of flirting with him through sarcasm.

"They just don't make 'em with much patience anymore do they?" He chuckled to himself and continued. "Well, why don't I teach you a bit of patience and answer the last question first, huh?"

We had long ago stopped playing cards. He more so just shuffled them in his hands periodically to stay occupied. I fidgeted with my hands as he told the story. I quickly learned to play with my own clothing instead of what was around me, like the table. Making the mistake of putting of rubbing my hands underneath the tabletop taught me quickly to keep them to myself. I tried hard not to gag when I realized there was gum covering the entire underside. Some pieces seemed to be a bit too fresh for my liking, the moist rubbery texture against my fingertips was enough to bring up this morning's breakfast.

"Those two months, like I said, were a breeze. Sure, it could be a little frustrating, especially when I saw some of the same folks over and over again. In my mind they had the opportunity to quit. But then there was a day.

I went in that day and saw that Hubert was the first on my appointment schedule. In fact, he was the only appointment I had that day. Hubert was a short, stocky guy. His hair line was receding, but his beard was full and red. He was put together well enough for you to know he valued his job, but not so much that he came off as a kiss ass. I could tell from his appearance alone that he valued the benefits of the job, but he was tired.

SIX

He walked in that day with khaki pants, not the dress kind, the utility kind. The ones that almost look like they should be wrinkled but they aren't. He had on a long sleeve button up. It was almost like denim, but not actually denim material. I always knew when Hubert was coming in because you could smell him a mile away. He doused himself in cologne daily, probably to hide the tiny scent of alcohol residue from the night before. It was a rather spicy scent. If you weren't careful, you'd suddenly feel as if pepper had been spilled directly inside your nostrils. The ironic thing about it, he put on so much it magnified the scent of his alcohol. You suddenly found yourself searching for any other scent to focus on around Hubert, otherwise you'd probably suffocate on him."

I chuckled at that description. I knew that scent all too well. My grandfather had a cologne that smelled nice, but if he accidentally put too much on, spicy was exactly how he smelled.

"Sometimes, I really enjoyed hearing my clients because they were actually quite funny. As a professional, it would definitely have been inappropriate to laugh at them in that moment, but in hindsight, some of them made my insides smile from time to time. When Hubert left my office that day, he also left me with a plethora of emotions."

"Doesn't all of this fall under confidentiality?" I asked curiously. I could tell he was about to share with me exactly how that session with Hubert went, but I awkwardly felt like I was about to hear something I shouldn't.

"Sweetheart, I'm in an insane asylum. You have no idea who Hubert is or where he is, and even if you did, what are they going to do to me at this point? Would anyone even believe you? That's one of the silver linings of being in such a place. I can really tell all the stories I want, and no one truly believes you if it's repeated."

"So, for all I know you could be lying to me right now. This could all be a figment of your imagination."

"It could be. That means either you really like fake stories, or you believe me. Otherwise, you would have gone to find Candy by now, whose probably somewhere screwing Jake."

"Who is Jake?"

"One of the orderlies. But anyway, do you want to hear the rest of the story or do ya think I'm lying."

I wasn't sure if I believed him, but for some reason I felt like I did. He seemed trustworthy enough. A few fly away pieces of hair fell in front of my face as I nodded for him to continue.

"That day, Hubert had a lot to say. I was pretty laid back. You were really only supposed to talk about workplace stresses with me, but I quickly began to realize that if the job was as stressful as these folks made it seem in their sessions, I was one of the only outlets they had: Who was I to tell them they couldn't get a little side advice? No one was checking in on the sessions anyway so, no harm no foul.

Hubert was a mix of emotions. He seemed happy, almost excited. But at the same time, he was nervous. Those weren't typically the first emotions I picked up from the people who came into my office. Especially Hubert, he was always a sweaty mess of frustration by the time he got to me. This time he was oddly, calm. Maybe that was it, it's at least the best word I can use to describe it anyway. That's not the point though.

Hubert came in that day talking a million miles a minute. I made it a habit not to interrupt clients when they spoke, but I had to butt in to ask him to slow down."

"Was it the job that had him all discombobulated?" I interjected; not sure I was fully following what he was saying.

"Actually, that time it wasn't. Not fully anyway. Basically, Hubert told me about this fling he had started…"

"Fling?!" If the use of that word wasn't bad enough, I definitely added to the theatrics of where we were in the conversation. I didn't intend to speak as loud as I did, wasn't even sure why it shocked me. Either way, the word flew out of my mouth in a bit of a high pitched squeal.

SIX

"Yeah, he was married, and we had talked plenty of times before about how the stress of his job was causing a strain in his marriage. He would leave work so frustrated and exhausted that he started an unhealthy drinking habit. There was a bar a few miles away from the facility that he would stop in everyday when he got off. One drink turned into four and before he knew it, he would have multiple missed calls from his wife. His job had really propelled him into a downward spiral that we were trying to work on. It was a slow process. Very slow.

The one thing I probably disliked the most about that job was that sessions were very limited because employees were allowed to come to them during work hours. That also meant the staff would be a little short during that time and they didn't want them gone for too long. I found that oddly ironic considering they wanted to keep them enough to offer counseling during shifts but didn't want to let them miss too much of that shift to try to get proper help.

Hubert was a prime example of someone who needed more session time. The stress of the job had created an alcohol addiction that was spiraling out of control. He was an employee who had been there for just three years or so and in that short amount of time, he had developed a crippling habit that was directly correlated with the strain his job was causing."

Even though his accent was filled with a country twang and he spoke in broken English sometimes, he definitely seemed to have the knowledge he said he had. For a lack of better viewpoint, he sounded quite educated in the field.

"So how did this fling affect him and his job?" Curiosity had long since gotten the best of me.

"Right. Well, he comes in that day and is, I guess you could say, relieved. He rattled on for a few moments about the stress of work, but then he suddenly said, 'But you know what Doc, it's okay because I won't be in this situation much longer.'

I didn't quite know what he meant, but I was sure he was going to continue so I stayed quiet a few moments longer. Sure enough, he told me everything.

'Doc, I know it's probably not the best thang to do, but man, I haven't felt this good in a long time. I feel, serene. I don't even know if that's the right word, I don't thank I've ever used it in my life.'

I gently asked him to slow down and tell me what exactly he was referring to.

'Well, I been trying to cut back on going out to the bar like you told me. So, I only try to go about two times a week now, instead of every day. I guess my wife likes that, but when I get home, I still feel empty. Anyways, the other day after work I decided to head over to the bar and bumped into a coworker. She works in a different department. She started telling me all about how terrible it is, and she wanted to find a way out, but her financial situation wouldn't let her.

The next thing I knew we were talking for hours and we came up with a plan to run away together.'"

"Run away together?! He'd just met her, and he was talking about running away with her and leaving his wife? Because of the stress of a job? That's The rage exploded inside me as if it were a volcano finally ready to erupt. My blood seemed to boil, and with every word coming out of my mouth I got louder and louder.. It was the most absurd thing I had ever heard, a man randomly leaving his family after one conversation.

I'm sure my anger stemmed from my own issues that had absolutely nothing to do with Lebannon or his counseling skills, but what came to mind came out in that moment. I didn't want to think about what I had seen a close friend go through in her marriage, but all of my emotions about her situation came flooding past the self control I had built, spilling out of my mouth in opposition of the man in front of me.

"Well sweetheart, I'd be inclined to agree if I didn't know the extent of stress this job put on folks. But I've already told you that I was only given so much time with them a session. I couldn't possibly unpack everything there was to unpack and properly counsel them in such short amount of time. I was a pretty smart grad student, but I won't ever a miracle worker." His tone didn't match mine. It didn't help that the country accent made everything he said warmer than he probably meant it. Suddenly, my rage flushed away as quickly as it had rushed in. I felt nervous

SIX

and embarrassed for my outburst in front of him. Not sure if that was from a lack of professionalism, or fear of him pulling back his flirtations. I went with the former as the latter was absurdly ridiculous.

"You're right. I'm sorry. Please, continue."

"Don't be sorry. Quite frankly, I didn't hear anything else Hubert said after that either. I was quite enraged myself."

"Really?"

"Yeah. Looking back that was probably one of the few moments I felt like I failed as a therapist. I allowed my own personal issues to get in the way of hearing the client out. Ya see Ella, my daddy ran out on my momma when I was a youngin'. It hurt like hell, but I could have lived with it. It was the trail of men Momma started leaving behind her that hurt worse. Once Daddy left, for some bimbo at a strip club no less, Momma started drowning her sorrows in cheap vodka and men. She had lost any standard she had for men when my daddy left, which meant the caliber of men she brought home were worse for me.

Some were nice enough, others not so much. I didn't have a therapist to go to and work my crap out when I was younger. I can't help but believe that was one of the reasons why I went into the Psychology field. It was the same ole sob story everyone has, and in that session with Hubert, I let it get in the way.

I'm pretty sure I just let Hubert go on and on about his new love interest and how they were running away together. Later on, I would regret that I didn't take more time to intently listen to what he was saying. I should have paid attention to the words he was using, but I was so angry. I was hurt for his wife. I couldn't possibly imagine a job being so terrible that I let it ruin my entire life that way. I wanted to know more about the job, but it was in my job description not to inquire of the employees. At that point, I was done anyway.

Hubert walked out with a smile that day, I think. I never saw him again."

SEVEN

There was a dramatic pause that took forever to subside. I was picking up that Lebannon had a taste for dramatics. I wasn't sure if that made his story more interesting, or the sense of dread that was coming heighten. Either way, I couldn't take the silence anymore. It was deafening.

"I appreciate how candid you were with that story, but what did that have to do with Claire?"

He smiled wide, "Why Miss Ella, if I didn't know any better, I would say you were getting a tad annoyed with me, hun." His tone was sweet and warm, instantly calming the little annoyance I hadn't realized was forming inside me.

"I'm not annoyed," I said with a sigh. "We've been sitting here talking for I'm not even sure how long and so far, I've only learned that you had a terrible childhood, and you can play a good game of cards. If I may be blunt, Lebannon."

"Touché' Miss Ella, touché." He shuffled the deck of cards a few times, then handed it over to me. "Here, why don't you do the shuffling to give you something to focus on. My story, I tell it in my timing. Unless you don't want to hear it anymore."

I rolled my eyes, snatching the deck of cards out of his hand. His smile was contagious, and I felt the tiny negative feelings of frustration and annoyance dwindle under it. I can't even count the number of times I completely forgot I was sitting across from a patient in a psychiatric facility. It was more like a random encounter with a stranger in a public place. He was so... Normal. Actually, he wasn't normal. He was charming and oddly relatable. He at least knew how to draw you in. At bare minimum, he was a great storyteller.

"I told you I was pretty upset with Hubert's declaration. He was the only client I had that day and one of the perks of the job was I came in to see the clients on the schedule. After those sessions were done, I was free to leave for the day, I just stayed on call until around five or so for any potential emergency situations. During those two months I'd never had an emergency situation come up." He kept adding air quotations around "emergency situation" as if he didn't know what one would have constituted.

"Once Hubert left my office, I packed my briefcase and headed down the grand stairwell. They had an elevator but since no one else ever seemed to use it, I wasn't going to try my luck with it. Oh, did I forget to mention this was my last week as an intern? I had two more days of internship, and I was sure the next day Mr. Linguh would be strolling into my office to offer me the permanent position. It wasn't like there were any other candidates no way. I was the only intern.

I was walkin' past Claire's desk when she stopped me in my tracks.

'Why the long face handsome, Hube piss in your cheerios or something?' She giggled and man did it warm my heart. I was still upset, but there was something about her giggle that made my heart smile, pushing all of those negative memories to the side for a moment.

I smiled back at her saying something sly, probably along the lines of something like that.

'I have an early day today, want to go grab brunch?'

She was asking me out. Man, I couldn't help but think I had really taken too long with that one because that pretty lady asked me out. I didn't think too much into it at the moment, but I sure was excited. I wanted to stay as professional as possible to ensure I got the job, but we did have a habit of flirting a little every day. She let me know she got off in about thirty more minutes, and I let her know I'd stick around and wait for her."

"What a gentleman," I teased.

"Hey, they can't all be like me can they?" He chuckled at his own notion.

"I guess not," I shuffled the deck of cards in front of me. They were helping me focus on something instead of fidgeting.

"I'll never forget how beautiful it was outside that day. It was overcast, the kind of clouds in the winter time that reminded you of snow. I know most people think of a bright sunny day when you refer to it as beautiful, but I love the overcast skies. I've always felt like it takes a special kind of person to appreciate the days everyone else looks down on.

It was chilly, but nothing a jacket couldn't fix. There was a large porch like area to the right side of the entrance. It was immaculate really, definitely something an ole country boy like myself could only dream of. I sat out there in a light gray rocking chair. It had a small cushion on it so your bottom didn't get sore. I sat my briefcase down beside me and before I knew it I was rocking.

Back and forth, back and forth. I couldn't help but wonder what better time to sit and reflect. Graduation was quickly approaching, I had been working my tail off and was confident I would soon be offered a job with all the benefits and everything would work out. In that moment I couldn't help but take in where I was. My emotions were all over the place but I picked one thing and just focused.

The wind. The wind was my one thing. I closed my eyes, took a deep breath, and appreciated the sudden rush of cool air filling my nostrils stretching down to my lungs. It was as if 1,000 tiny little pins were fighting their way into my nostrils trying to be the first to my lungs as the finish line. It was refreshing. I felt like it had been the first deep breath I had taken in a while. It was amazing. I foolishly sat there, starin' at the darkness behind my eyelids, wondering if I could feel more of that moment."

His recollection was beautiful. Probably another reason why I easily forgot the person I was an audience for was a patient, with some mental illness. I was supposed to be trying to figure his symptoms out, but I couldn't help but believe there was potential behind the conspiracy theory he said put him there. He was too articulate, too poised. I had long abandoned the idea of separating symptoms from behaviors and personality. Now it was all about hearing the story.

"The moment passed too quick. I'm not sure if I dosed off for a little catnap, or if I just became so enthralled in the moment that I lost track of time. The next thang I remember, Claire was tappin' me on the shoulder. She made a joke about me being exhausted.

She was gorgeous. Her hair flowed effortlessly, hanging down in front of her face as she bent over in front of me. I shuffled in the chair, grabbed my briefcase, and exhaled all the little pins I had inhaled thirty minutes earlier. Then we headed on to get brunch. I offered to drive us both but she insisted we take our own cars since the facility was so far out of the way. She didn't want me to have to bring her all the way back to her car, so I followed her to a local favorite."

I realized there was a small subtle change in his tone from time to time. It wasn't really his tone, maybe more of his accent. At times it seemed his southern drawl was exaggerated, others it seemed barely noticeable. I shrugged it off, thinking his accent may just become more or less apparent depending on what he was talking about or what emotion he was feeling. That could have been a small indication of whatever mental health struggle that kept him bound in that facility, I didn't count on it though. Everything about him was normal; uncanny and normal.

EIGHT

"So," I started, filling a long silent pause as usual. He had a habit of trailing off in the middle of his story, typically as he transitioned into a new part. It was almost as if he was recalling it in his mind, before he said it out loud. Trying hard to remember what happened next. "How was brunch? I don't know what stressed workers eat for brunch, but I have a few classmates who love eating chicken and waffles."

"Actually, that's what she had. I'm more of a french toast and grits guy myself."

"Shrimp and grits?"

"Is there any other way?" His smile caught me off guard. It was charming. For a split second I thought he was flirting with me. I quickly dismissed that thought as irrational. There was just something about those pearly white teeth, peaking from behind his well moisturized lips. There was that sparkle again, briefly lighting a small flame inside of me.

"Well," I said, finding myself smiling back. "How was the rest of the date? Or did you eat in silence." It was sarcastic, snarky. I tried not to be too sarcastic often, but something about him brought sarcasm out of me. Was that how we flirted with one another? Was sarcasm somehow attractive fror him?

"Actually, that's where things became interestin'."

"Oh!" I said with surprise, "Interesting eh?"

"Yeah," he chuckled at my enthusiasm. "I'm sure it's not the kind of interesting you may think though."

He had my attention yet again. I was on the edge of my seat, interested to know more about how Claire felt about him. My mind was filled with questions. *What happened with them? Did they ever make it in a relationship? And where was she now? Did she know about his mental health struggles? Maybe she couldn't take it.* I figured the more I knew about how Claire responded to him, the more I might know about the kind of person he really was. But I was getting ahead of myself. Not to mention surely he would tell the story the way he wanted it told, leaving a few key details out. He continued on with the story.

"Claire was great! Her company really was better than I could have imagined. Talking to her was effortless, unlike anything I had ever experienced really. Sometimes, my accent has a way of making it hard for people to understand me, but not one time did she ask me to repeat myself.

'Why did you seem so upset after your session with Hubert earlier? Did he tell you about his fling with Jin?'

I can't lie to ya Ella, she caught me clear off guard with that one. I thought I had found out something in confidence, but obviously Claire already knew!

'Don't look at me with such shock,' she smiled, stuffing her mouth with a piece of chicken dripping in honey. 'Honestly, most of the people you see in sessions, talk to me too. You're the professional; I'm just the one they vent to. I probably know everything about everybody in there.'

She wasn't saying it in a boastful way, and I didn't get the notion that she was a gossip. I knew she was the secretary, and she was pretty; why wouldn't people confide in her? Quite frankly I was relieved, I didn't want to hide what I was feeling, but I also didn't want to break client confidentiality."

"Like you're doing now?" I interjected half jokingly. He continued, ignoring me.

EIGHT

"We talked a bit about how I didn't understand men who could just give up on their families, but somewhere along the way the conversation took a turn. Before I knew it, we were down a long dirt road with only one lane.

'I'm pretty sure I'm going to be offered the permanent position this week. It's my last week interning.' I was so excited when I said it to her. She didn't seem to feel the same though. Her eyebrows furrowed and her smile suddenly faded into a grim sadness. I had never really seen an actual frown on someone before, ya know like in the cartoons when their lips twist downward. Yeah, that's what she did. Soon she had gone quiet, focusing only on the honey drizzled across her plate. I couldn't quite wrap my mind around why she wasn't excited. Of course I knew it was a stressful place for other workers, but my job wasn't stressful at all. She was always smiling too so I didn't get it.

'Don't take the job.' It caught me off guard. I had just put a big ole spoonful of grits in my mouth. Forgetting just that quick, I gasped slightly, inhaling a combination of grits and Cajun sauce at the same time. Nearly choked to death right in front of her."

He had started to say my name more often in conversation. It was personable but a little weird. It was really unnecessary, I was already engaged in the conversation, there was no need to try to keep me interested. I was already there. Maybe it was only weird because everytime he said my name, the small little flame inside me seemed to burn a little brighter. I didn't know how to respond to the sudden shift in my breathing as I tried to calmly blow out the flame from the outside in.

"I'm pretty sure I startled her with all my coughin. I could only imagine a combination of shock and confusion twisted together was plastered on my face when I finally got my bearings together. The cup of juice was cold, slightly moist in my hand as I picked it up to take a sip. I realized that her beautiful laugh had been substituted for a more concerned, almost sad look.

'What's wrong? Why would you tell me not to take the job?'

'You don't really know what you're getting into Lebannon. It's not what you think it is. What you're doing now is just to get you in the door. The job they are going to offer you is going to kill you.'

I was utterly confused. My stomach dropped and I slowly lowered the spoon holding my next bite of grits down into the bowl. 'I don't understand Claire, what are you talkin' about?'

There was a long sigh as she looked down at her food, pushing the syrup towards the honey back and forth across her plate. 'Listen Lebannon, I really like you. You're so sweet and nice, I enjoy flirting with you everyday, but that smile of yours, it would go away.'

I just sat there, waiting for her to go on. 'The benefits are great, I know. But trust me, the job isn't going to be worth what you're going to be doing.'

'What exactly is it that I'm going to be doing, Claire? And what's the deal with this job anyway, why is everyone always so miserable? How stressful can this place be?'

'Well, the reality is the facility is a web center. Every person has a job that's pretty much a need to know description of what they do. Each department does one thing or another for the dark web.'

'The dark web?!' I couldn't hide my shock.

'Yes. The entire facility runs on our ability to cater to the types of people who lurk in the shadows of the places most normal people don't even know exist on the internet. For instance, Hubert works in the L department. His department is responsible for monitoring the sites across the dark web that deal directly with child pornography. They have to see those images and conversations daily in order to ensure they can circumvent anything that could put those webbers in jeopardy of no longer spending their money there.'

I was absolutely horrified."

"You were horrified?!" I interrupted hysterically. "What the... You mean the facility was basically the house for the dark web and making sure perverts and other online criminals stay unscathed?"

EIGHT

"Yes'm that was how I was taking it to, and believe it or not I had the same reaction as you. I was just quiet. I sat there staring at her for the longest, and then I asked the same question you did. 'So you mean to tell me,'

'Shhhh!' She looked from side to side around us in the restaurant, peering out the side of her eyes to ensure there wasn't anyone sitting in the booth behind us. 'Not so loud, you're not really supposed to know until Mr. Linguh tells you. He's nice enough, but you don't want to cross him, trust me. Not to mention, the work done there isn't really conversation for everyone in a restaurant to here.'

I followed the motions of her head, mimicking her with my own sudden insecurity of how loud I was talking and who was around. Lowering my voice, I tried again; 'You're telling me, that for the last few weeks I have been working in the middle of the dark web? And I'm no more the wiser?' I was confused. Shocked. Dumbfounded. I wasn't sure if I was more upset about the content of the type of facility I was working in or that I had no idea. I was pretty sure it was the latter.

Saying this out loud, all these years later, I have to admit that I was more amazed that I could be a therapist and not realize the type of establishment willing to employ me. I'm honestly quite a bit amazed at how well everyone, with the exception of Claire, kept their mouth closed to those who weren't supposed to know. What could the consequence possibly have been? Most of them were fairly miserable. Based on my understanding, there were a large number of employees working in different departments throughout the facility. It's quite immaculate that they could get all of those employees to keep quiet. Who doesn't gossip a little from time to time?"

This was where one of his long pauses came in. This time though, I appreciated it. I had to take in everything that he was saying. The dark web. Child pornography. No wonder people were so stressed out, those types of things did indeed mess with the morality of a person. This was probably especially true for people who were working to ensure these spaces were safe for these types of criminals to do whatever it was they were doing.

Suddenly I found myself uncomfortable. It was as if a cover had been ripped off of me and I was now exposed to the world. I couldn't help but feel as if I wanted to grasp at the air to try to find that invisible blanket and cover myself back up. Of course I knew there were things people did out there in the world that were less than humane. I even knew there was potential in the career field I was pursuing for me to come across such individuals; but I would have never thought about anything like this.

The dark web wasn't unbeknownst to me. Everyone knows about it. I guess I never considered it being facilitated by one organization to keep things running smoothly. A pool of space available for the like minded. No wonder they could afford to have benefits as good as the ones Lebannon says enticed him. It had to be a lucrative business.

Lebannon cleared his throat, reaching at an imaginary tie adjusting the collar on his shirt. "Claire didn't go into much more detail about what I'd be doing specifically," he started. "She got quite for a while, we both picked at our food and then asked for the check.

'Lebannon, I really like you. It's pretty blunt and straightforward, but what can I say. I can tell you like me too which is why I'm asking you to decline the job offer.'

'Claire, I do really like you. You are absolutely beautiful. I don't know what you risked telling me the things you did, and I know it must be very important for you, but I have to think about this.'

'I completely understand. Call me later?' She was inquisitive with her question. She had been blunt and I could tell despite the information she shared and request she posed; she wanted reciprocation of her feelings towards me.

'Sure will, sweetheart,' I kissed her on her forehead and we went our separate ways. I remember wondering if that was why she'd pushed for us to drive our own cars, to skip an awkward car ride after brunch."

NINE

"Does Candy always go MIA during the workday?" I asked. I had spent a long time sitting there with Lebannon and Candy still hadn't come to find me. I was genuinely curious about where she could be and how this could affect today's assignment. More so though, I was at the point where I didn't know what I would do if she pulled me to do something before Lebannon finished his story.

"Candy can be quite forgetful. She's basically the glue that keeps this place running, but with that comes the ability to do whatever she wants. I wouldn't be surprised if she completely forgot you were in here. If you're waitin' on her to come back and get you, you'll probably be waitin' for a while longer, less of course you go huntin' for her on your own."

"Oh. Okay," I tried to sound as monotone as possible. I didn't want him to think I was too excited to continue sitting there with him. Wouldn't have wanted him to get the wrong idea. I also didn't want to seem disappointed in the news and risk offending him. That was what my life, in that moment, had come to. If I had a guy grab my attention, for any reason, the way Lebannon did, I probably wouldn't be single.

TEN

"I had a few projects to finish up that day, so being able to leave the office early made things easy. I tried as best I could to get last minute things turned in and prepared for graduation. Anything I could do to keep my mind off the things Claire had shared with me. It worked, for a while. Once I settled down that night though, I had to face it all."

He sounded weary, sincere almost. It was as if he was recalling a time of great turmoil. For a split second I felt sorry for him.

"Ella, I laid my head on my pillow that night and it was as if the pillow was a key that unlocked the door I had been trying so hard to keep shut all day. Suddenly I was there in the dark, watching all my recollections and concerns pour out across my eyelids.

I never considered myself to be immoral, but at the same time I didn't know how much certain things could really affect me. I had already been through a lot as a kid, and I felt like I made it alright. Havin' to go through what I did with some of the men my momma brought home was hard for me. I had built up some walls, some pretty hefty walls. I dealt with it my way and had convinced myself I'd do whatever I could to meet my goals.

The reality was, there in the darkness of my room, I was deep in debt and I had a way out. The benefits that I already had wind of were too great. Not to mention, I surely wasn't going to be working in the same capacity as other employees. I was the therapist. How much different could the permanent position be from what I had already been doing?

I was somewhat torn. I didn't like the sound of my employer basically being a filter for all of the bad things that happened. But if I'm to be totally honest with you here, I wasn't trying to be Mr. Save the World. No matter if I took the job or not, I wouldn't be doing anything more to stop what was happenin'. Best I could figure was depending on how much the pay was they offered me, I could work long enough to get ahead in life. If it was as terrible as other people made it out to be, I would quit once I had saved up enough. Not to mention, I really needed them to take care of my student loans.

I'm telling it to you like it was something I came to lightly, but if I am tellin' you the truth, I laid there in my bed for hours. Laying there, pitch black behind my eyelids, the other side just as dark. Playing all the what ifs in my head over and over and over again. What it all came down to, all the what-ifs, was that if the money was good enough I didn't see why I should pass up the opportunity."

The sadness that rolled out with each word he spoke was daunting. Almost as contagious as his laugh. I could tell that night must have been extremely conflicting for him. I couldn't really imagine what I would do if I were faced with that type of dilemma. In my mind I'd like to think that I would do the most morally acceptable thing for my conscious. Something deep inside me however told me that if I were faced with financial struggles that caused that type of stress and uncertainty, I'd probably look the other way long enough to alleviate my problems too.

"It was late, and I didn't want to give the wrong impression, but something told me it would be fine. It was after midnight. My momma didn't teach me a whole lot of thangs before Daddy left, but she did teach me not to call no woman after ten. But I did it anyway that night.

'I was starting to think you weren't going to call,' her voice was so sweet on the other end of the phone. It was a little hushed, you know how you women are. But there was just enough light in her voice to

TEN

shine through the phone and alleviate the pitch black that had been the background for my thoughts.

'Well, I did tell ya I was gone call, didn't I?'

'You did. Honestly didn't think you were though. I kind of dropped a lot on you today.'

'Yeah, that's why it's so late. I've been laying here thinking about that for a while now.

'What did you come up with?'

'Claire, I gotta be honest with you. I don't know about your life, but I've had quite the go of mine. With that being said, I have come to understand the financial gain of working at this here place is too large for me to pass up. I've told myself that I at least need to hear out what the job description is and what the financial benefit is. Worst-case scenario, I stick it out until I can make sure my head is above water after graduation.

I know you don't want me to take it, but I have to think about my financial well-being. I've been through a lot and me not taking the job wouldn't stop the facility from doing what their doing, I might as well try to get ahead while I can.' She was quiet for a minute. 'Hello?'

'I'm still here. I can't say that I'm all that thrilled to hear you say that, but it would be foolish and hypocritical of me to say I didn't understand. I mean, I still work there myself. Though what I do is different from what you'll do, I work there just the same. I just don't want you to be changed the way I've seen other people change who have come through there.'

I chuckled to myself, trying to be smooth. I was tired of thinking and talking about all of it frankly. I wanted to wait and see what happened whenever Mr. Linguh approached me. Keeping that in mind, but not wanting to get off the phone with her just yet, I said, 'Well sugar it sounds like you think you know me. What if I ain't as morally sound as you think I am.' I smiled when I said it, because I thought it was the perfect way to change the subject and flirt a little along the way. Man did I think I was smooth back then.

It worked. We started talking about other random things as if we were two teenagers. It was well past midnight and I was on the phone with a girl, getting to know her. Before I knew it I had turned the lights on in my room. I was pacing, I just couldn't seem to sit still. I would sit at the edge of my bed on the floor, and then lay across the floor. I couldn't even tell ya how many different times I moved while we were on that phone. But I was loving every minute of it."

"That was really some high school stuff, huh?" I interrupted, smiling at my own remembrance of staying up late on the phone with guys I liked. Suddenly I felt a rush of nostalgia come crashing over me like a wave at the thought. It was short lived though, another rolling wave of sadness followed, realizing those were some of the best times of my life. Back when everything was simple, and I was carefree.

"Oh yeah. Once we were on a roll, we were on a roll. It felt great to just talk to someone. I hadn't really allowed myself to be that free with anyone. I didn't know why I was being that way with her then, but I enjoyed the feeling. A lot.

By the time we got off the phone, the sun was just starting to peak over the horizon. She had to be at work in about two hours, and I had to be there in three. We were going to be exhausted."

"Did you think your decision to take the job would affect how you and Claire's relationship proceeded?" I was curious. I hadn't bothered to entertain many men, and it wasn't really on my mind that day either. I was more of a fling now, long-term relationship later kind of girl. I was more focused on my own career. "I mean, were you even looking for a relationship for it to make that much of a difference anyway?"

"I've never just been on the hunt for a relationship. They take work, a lot of work. Especially when it comes to someone with as much childhood trauma as me. However, that never did stop me. The way I saw it,

TEN

and still do really, if a person grabs my attention and we can click, why not give it a try?

I wasn't really looking for a relationship with Claire, but I wasn't opposed to one either. Of course her opinion alone didn't hold enough weight to matter when it came to my decision to accept a job offer. The things she said came into consideration, but her reasoning alone wasn't enough. We'd had one date, and yes we had clicked, but if I had to choose her over my financial future, it was a no brainer at that point.

I find myself wondering if it would have been different. If we went out when I first started internship, would her concerns have held more weight. On paper, two months doesn't seem like long enough for someone's opinion to hold so much weight it can affect the future of another. And yeah, my childhood was terrible, but I still held on to enough hope to believe and know that love really could escalate quickly."

"You're probably the first person I've ever met that still has such high hope in love after experiencing what you did with your mom and dad." It was true. Everyone I knew, male and female, that faced big challenges like that as a child all had trouble believing in love.

"Yeah well, like I said, I dealt with a lot myself. At some point I realized my perspective on things was going to determine how happy I allowed myself to be in life. Because of that, I try my damnest to remember what Momma and Daddy were like before he left. That was what I wanted, no matter if it just looked like that to tiny me or was reality. That part don't matter."

"That's admirable to say the least."

"If this story wasn't so detailed, I might ask you what you think about love. But you seem like the type who just has flings and a career."

How did he know that?

"Anyway, about an hour after I finally fell asleep, my alarm was blarin' at me to wake up. I thought I would be exhausted. And yeah, it took me a few more minutes than it normally would to wake on up, but

I actually felt... refreshed. I was kind of excited to see Claire. I felt like a high school kid who couldn't wait to pass his crush in the hallway.

I always took pride in my appearance. Especially given the fact that I started on a mission to get a full time job when it was all said and done. I took a little extra care that day though. I had pulled out my laptop to check my schedule and realized my first session, which should have been with Hubert, was cancelled. That meant I had an extra hour to get ready and get out to my office. Suddenly I wanted to impress her. I put on my best dress clothes. By best, I mean the snazziest shirts I had from thrifting over the past few months. I even pulled out my Sunday cologne...."

"Sunday cologne?" I stopped him mid sentence. "Why would you have Sunday cologne, I thought you weren't religious."

"Well I'm not, but my folks were for a little while. I knew that Daddy had a cologne he wore only on Sunday's to church and special occasions. He called it his Sunday cologne, so I followed suit as an adult. It's just the word I learned to substitute for special specifically for cologne."

I felt my lips curl down in interest and somewhat shock. I couldn't help but to again think that this man, thus far, had showed no indication of a mental illness that would land him in there. If I were to allow the thought to become an actual recollection, I was sitting there thinking wow; this seemed like the perfect kind of guy if we were beyond the walls of that asylum.

"I put so much effort and thought into impressing Claire that day," he interrupted my intrigue of his cologne explanation. "I had almost forgotten that I was halfway expecting Mr. Linguh to offer me the job that day. I had completely forgotten I was on my last few days of internship and there was a small potential I wouldn't be going in to work and seeing Claire anymore. But that was all resolved later in the day when Mr. Linguh walked in once my last session left."

ELEVEN

"I didn't take all of my extra time to get ready. Instead, I left the house early enough to stop and get a couple coffees, one for me and one for Claire. I didn't really know what she liked, but I did know she liked sweet. So I asked the barista to pick for me and headed out to the facility.

She acted as if I had brought her flowers and chocolates on Valentine's Day. Boy you shoulda seen the way she lit up. I don't know if she actually liked the coffee or not, but she seemed to genuinely appreciate it nonetheless. That made me happy. Giddy would actually be a better depiction of what I felt.

We flirted for a minute, then I started up the stairs to my office. I only had two sessions on the calendar so far, since Hubert canceled. It was going to be a light day. In the back of my mind though, I wondered what happened to Hubert. Had he seriously ran off with some girl?"

Everytime he talked about Claire, something was different. This time it was a complete 180 from when he explained that night he was trying to figure out what to do. His recollection of things with her was even a little different than when he recalled their brunch date. This seemed, from the outside looking in on a memory, to have been a love connection. I hate to admit this, but for a split second there was a little tinge of jealousy. He didn't at all flirt with me when he talked about Claire. Oh how ridiculous I was.

There was still so much to unpack about this man and his circumstances. Obviously at some point in his life he had someone, so where was she now? And I still didn't know what his job had to do with him being in that asylum, though it could make sense. Working at the type of place that ensured the dark places of the world continued to run smoothly and unscathed sounded risky, and potentially dangerous based on the many crime shows I watched in my life.

"What happened when Mr. Linguh came in?" I didn't feel like risking the fact that he might tell me about those two employee sessions. That wasn't what I cared about. Mr. Linguh was the start of how all this tied together. I wanted to jump straight there.

"As soon as my last session left, I mean as soon as the door opened, Mr. Linguh came in. It startled Sands a little bit. He was the guy in my second session. I mean I sure wouldn't want to feel like the big dog had been sitting on the other side of my therapy session. As Sands hurried away, Mr. Linguh came in, shutting the door behind him. He had a big grin on his face.

'Lebannon, how are things going for ya?' He was chipper, that wasn't something I had ever seen from him. He held a large folder in his hand and sat promptly across from my desk.

'I'm doin quite well, Mr. Linguh. What about you?'

'Oh I'm peachy I'd say, just peachy. Hey listen, you have been doing great these last few weeks. I've heard nothing but great things from the surveys we send out to those who need therapy, and overall I'm extremely pleased with what you've accomplished thus far.'

'Why thank you, sir. I really appreciate that.' I admit, this was a little weirder than I expected. Looking at Mr. Linguh I wouldn't dare have imagined words like "peachy" were even in his vocabulary. He was being extraordinarily nice and it honestly was an awkward fit for him. I started to realize that this was what I had been waiting two months for. Now I was eagerly waiting to get all of the information I could. I wanted to fill in the blanks Claire'd left out.

ELEVEN

'I know graduation isn't for another month or so, but I want to extend the offer to employ you permanently here with us. I know you still have a bit of a school schedule, but I could work something out with your professor who is a good friend of mine. I would love for you to start in your new position as soon as tomorrow.'

I was flattered, but I wasn't dumb. And based on the conversation I had with Claire, I wasn't going to blindly accept without getting all of the information I could. 'I would absolutely love to Mr. Linguh,' I started with the most professional tone and vocabulary I could muster. 'Though while I'd love to accept the offer, I feel inclined to ensure that this will be the best fit for me long term. I have been looking into all my potential employment options, and want to make sure I am setting myself up for success, both in my career and in my financial stability.'

I could tell by the look on his face he was impressed."

If I'm to be honest, I was impressed too. Men always had the confidence to say such things with employers, and I just never thought that would bode well for me as a female. I would have to try it one day, just to see what happens.

"He looked at me and smiled. 'I knew there was something about you, Lebannon. I appreciate your candidness. Of course you don't have to accept or make any decisions today, however I do not want to lose the potential asset you are to my company. Let me tell you a little bit about what this offer entails to help ease your mind.'

Bingo. That was exactly what I wanted him to say.

'Firstly, we do offer a plethora of benefits, to include dental and health insurance. We also take your mental health very seriously, as you can probably already tell. You would also have access to an outside therapist if need be. We don't expect you to counsel yourself, and we know even the best have the potential to need help from time to time. Additionally, we offer a student loan repayment program. I'm unaware if you have student loans or not, but we pay them for you; either half or in full. With that program, it does require a minimum commitment. You sign one of two contracts. Either you commit to employment for three months and we pay half your student loan balance, or you commit to a minimum of six months and we pay your entire balance. That is paid at the time you sign the contract, however I must warn that in the even you don't complete the contract, it then becomes a loan you have to pay back to us with interest.'

I was amazed. They could pay my entire student loan balance off today, and all I had to do was commit to six months. No matter what the job was, I was confident at that point that I would give six months of my life for my total loan balance to be paid off. That was about $90k! That alone had me jumpin' inside my skin wanting to blurt out a big YES! But I kept my composure and let him keep on talkin'.

'Listen,' the chair squeaked a little at the sudden shift of his weight as he leaned closer to my desk. 'I really need you. I don't say that lightly either. I've been trying to get this position filled since the last therapist didn't renew his contract. I'm in a position to make unbeatable offers. So, along with student loan help if you need it, your starting salary will be $110k for the length of your contract. Which means if you sign a six-month contract, you get $100,000 in six months time. After six months, assuming you stay committed that long, we will reevaluate and there's the potential for a raise in salary at that time. We also have a healthy pension packet and our retirement eligibility is significantly shorter than other industries out there, due to the nature of our work.'

I was floored. Completely floored. I knew about what to expect my starting salary to be after graduating. I even anticipated a little less. The figures that spewed out of his mouth were WAY over what I could have ever thought. Not to mention eliminating the largest debt I had, and benefits! There was absolutely no way I could pass that opportunity up. Just six months alone could drastically change my life. It was almost like winning the lottery. In my mind, what was six months? I could keep the morality I had together for six months, whatever I needed to get my

ELEVEN

debt paid and rack up a decent savings account. That opportunity was one in a million for a guy like me.

I sat back in my chair for a moment,.The game face I tried to portray prior to that moment had dissipated, replaced only by complete shock.

'Mr. Linguh, I've got to hand it to you, so far this is the best offer I've ever heard. With that being said, I am certainly confident I will be accepting your offer. Six months alone can drastically change my life if I may be candid with you, sir. You've told me a lot about what the benefits are, but I would be remised if I didn't inquire of you what the catch was. In the real world, employers don't offer that much money without wanting an arm and a leg in return. Now don't get me wrong, I'm not saying that will deter me from accepting, honestly I need to take advantage of this while I can, I'd just like to prepare myself for what I'm up against.'

He sat back a little and smirked, intertwining his fingers laying both hands across his chest. 'Lebannon, I have to admire you, son. You're the first person I've offered this position to who approached it the way you have. It's quite important to prepare yourself for your job and not just flock towards all the shiny things that are offered. This job is unique. Our facility isn't normal, and I'm sure, if my employees are adhering to their own agreements and contracts, you aren't too aware of what we really do around here. It's quite unorthodox, and I must warn that it does take a strong type of person to deal with what we deal with.

You see, Lebannon, I have built an empire on the sins and downfalls of others. Unfortunately, that means we see and deal with things that aren't the norm in society. In actuality it is all quite the opposite.'

'How do you mean?'

'Listen, I'm going to cut the dramatics and get down to it because I trust you are indeed going to accept my offer. Have you ever heard of the dark web?'

'You mean like where criminals and desperate people are able to get things they shouldn't? The illegal part of the internet?'

'Yes, that's the one. Well, this is it.' He held his arms up toward the ceiling as if making a grand gesture towards the facility. 'We are the dark web, more so, we house it. We have departments designed to monitor and keep up with any and all things dark web. Essentially protecting those who use it, no matter their reasoning. It is a rather immoral workplace for most people, and those who decide to accept employment are typically highly stressed because of the sudden conflict of their financial well being and their morality. But that's it. That's the big catch.'

It was finally out in the open. He had said it, in as little and as much detail as he could. I had already made up my mind, I was going to have to suck up any conflict long enough to get my chest above water. From there I would just have to see how it went.

'Mr. Linguh, I think there's a reason I was given an internship opportunity here. You've made an offer I would be absolutely fool to pass up, plus you can get me out of the last few weeks of class.' I joked. He laughed, catching on which relieved me. Didn't want to go making a complete fool of myself so soon. 'I'll be accepting your offer sir. And I'll be more than happy to start tomorrow in a permanent capacity.'

'Delighted Lebannon, simply delighted!' He jumped up quickly, startling me a bit. I stood up, following suit. His hand was outstretched for a congratulatory handshake. The large folder had been swiftly tucked under his arm as he got up and put out his hand for the handshake. It was all one fluid motion. After that handshake, a lot of paperwork followed. Then I was faced with the reality that Claire had tried so desperately to warn me about. There was no going back by then. Contracts had been signed.

TWELVE

Dramatic pause. I had come to expect it. If there were anything less than a dramatic pause in a turning point of his story, it wouldn't be Lebannon's story. He could have been an author or screen write. At minimum, he could have been an actor the way he included dramatics for affect. This one was needed though. We had finally were getting to the meat and potatoes of his story, and I needed a moment to catch my breath.

There was an explosion of duress coming from my lungs. I hadn't realized, but I had been holding my breath since he said Mr. Linguh walked in his office. I was on edge and anxious to see what was going to happen. I had so many questions, but I didn't want to interrupt and make the story drag on any further. I figured once he made it to the end I would ask all the most pertinent questions. Until then, I had to remember to breath. My lungs would hate me if I didn't.

At that point I was so curious about what all happened inside that facility. What did they really DO? I wasn't so much concerned about why everyone was so stressed, what Mr. Linguh said made complete sense. I could only imagine the raging conflict inside of someone once they started dealing with the kind of subject matter they were taught was wrong and repulsive. I also still had so many questions about Claire. I was stuck somewhere in between wanting to know about the love connection and wanting to know more about the terrible job that he said ruined his life.

Before I could finish prioritizing the questions, comments, and concerns racing around in my head Lebannon's twang was filling the room again. "The folder was filled with paperwork. NDA's, contract options, policies. I spent another thirty minutes there with Mr. Linguh, going over all the paperwork. Now that I'm saying it out loud, it was right odd. I mean, wasn't that the sort of thing HR did?

I had opted to do a six-month contract, allowing the company to pay 100% of my student loans off. Just like that, I had walked into an internship that morning and was going to be walking out not only employed, but student loan free.

It was quite surreal for a moment. Then I came across a document that said housing agreement. One of the perks Mr. Linguh hadn't mentioned, until we got to that form. Because of the position I was going to hold, I had a housing stipend. There was a private condo that I could move into for the duration of my contract, rent-free. The only thing I was responsible for would be my own food and entertainment. The condo apparently came fully furnished, with utilities completely covered. It was as if my pupils had turned into tiny dollar signs inside my head. Not only was I not going to have to pay student loans after graduation, but I also wouldn't have many needs that I'd have to pay for. My entire check could go towards saving, investing, and developing a standard of living I could only dream of."

"I may not be in the position you were in back then, but I must say all of this sounds too good to be true. Even so I probably would have taken advantage too. That is indeed like winning the lottery." I couldn't help myself. Those were the types of things that just didn't happen in the real world.

"You're absolutely right Miss Ella. I can assure you, it was too good to be true: Eventually.

My hand was cramping by the time I was done with all the paperwork. I had never signed my name so much in my life. I started to think I was spelling it wrong, it didn't look right anymore. As soon as I was

TWELVE

done, Mr. Linguh went into much more detail about what my position held and what expectations were before me.

'Let's go for a tour,' another swift uified motin as he got up fixing the button on his blazer.. 'Firstly, Lebannon, I want you to be completely aware that your position here is the most important there is. Even more important than mine I must admit. There are only a handful of people who know about each and every department in this facility. I've been doing this for some time and found that things run the best when other departments aren't aware of the functions of each other. You, Claire, Chelsty, and myself are among the few that are to be aware of the capacity each department holds. The only exception is that all employees, at some point or another are made aware of your position as well. At least that your assistance will be available.'

We left my office and started down a long corridor to the left. I was finally going through the large badge only doors. On the other side was a huge room. There were five different corridors, labeled accordingly. Each was also painted a different color, but all variations of reds and oranges. It was captivating, beautiful really, but a bit different than the elegant design I had become accustomed to the last two months. I had never been to this side of the building; there wasn't a reason to. All the employees came to me, and I was pretty close to the front entrance. As far as I was concerned, that was all that mattered to me."

"You never had a tour of the building? Never even wandered off?" I asked him, thinking about how large I thought the asylum was. Then I realized, I had only been the front of it too. And so far, I had plenty of time to explore and get lost, but I hadn't.

"There was never any reason too. I was never a super curious guy. When you go lookin' for stuff, you find stuff. I don't always feel like dealing with what may be found. I was finding stuff then though. Mr. Linguh kept on with his tour and explanations.

'You've already been around the administrative department. That's where you've done your internship so far. Those are the folks that everyone else is a little envious of.' He chuckled, obviously at an inside joke. 'There really isn't much to be envious of, but their requirements are minimal compared to other departments. It's kind of a running joke among the few of us who know all the departments.' He gathered his composure, trying to clear the laugh out of his throat and continued. That really seemed to tickle him. 'There are a total of seven different departments. Your department is one, which we will get to, and you've already been in admin. I am technically considered in admin. Down here are all of the other departments.'

People started to walk past us, some leaving the colored corridors, others going towards them. Some spoke to Mr. Linguh, others looked away and sped up their pace. There were suddenly more people walking past me than I felt I had ever seen in the two months I had been working there. It was as if I had suddenly walked into the middle of a mall, and stood right outside of the food court. The thought was ironic given Mr. Linguh's next sentence.

'Through this large walkway behind us is the cafeteria.' We started toward a pastel orange colored hallway. Walking down the hall it was lined with pictures and abstract pieces, all food related. It was wide, and smelled like a wonderful combination of cuisines. 'Folks call those workers the laziest because the only interaction they have as far as this place is concerned is with other employees.' His voice lowered a little. 'They honestly probably have the best go of it as far as job description goes, outside of the admin department that is. I guess it is rather envious to the other folks. Either way, you're free to eat as often and as much as you want. All of the food in the cafeteria is covered by a comp in your salary. Which kind of means it's free to you. They are staffed 24 hours and have everything you could ever want. We try to add as many perks as possible around here, given the nature of the job. Who doesn't love the ability to walk down and get as much free food as they want right?'

'Wow!' By the time he had posed that question, we passed the through to the cafeteria. It was unlike anything I had ever seen. The

TWELVE

college cafeteria was rinky dink compared to it. My mouth is watering just thinking about it. I had never seen such an amazing hub of food options. It wasn't like a standard cafeteria. It was more like a full gourmet food court. There was Italian, American, breakfast, dinner, buffet options, premade course options, Mexican; the options were literally endless. Anything you could think about was an option.

'Yeah, it's pretty great right?' Mr. Linguh interrupted my awe. 'If there's ever anything you want or are craving and you don't see it out here, there's a few machines throughout the cafeteria that allows you to put a custom order in. You will also have access to email in an order from your office to pick up or have one of the runners bring to you. You hungry?'

'Would it be weird if I said yes?' I mean, he did ask. I figured we were already doing things that were probably considered impolite or unorthodox for a somewhat interview. No need to neglect the hunger that suddenly struck my stomach.

'Absolutely not. I could go for a snack myself. Why don't we have a quick bite before finishing the tour.'

He picked up a yogurt and a bowl of fresh fruit. That looked good, but a bit too light and healthy for my taste. There was a station of New York style pizza that caught my eye. I grabbed a slice and a soda then found him at a table on the far end of the cafeteria. The chairs were unusually soft, not something you would expect in a food court or a cafeteria. That first bite was heavenly. I'm pretty sure I made some embarrassing noise because he laughed to himself, taking in a spoonful of yogurt.

The pizza crunched in my mouth, the crust was crisp and flavorful. It was buttery really, with a hint of parmesan and garlic. The combination of meats and cheeses came together with each time I chewed. I grabbed my napkin to wipe the grease that was flowing down my chin. I felt like I hadn't had anything that good in a while.

'My compliments to the chef,' my mouth was still full of food. I instinctually lifted my napkin to cover my mouth as I spoke, making sure he didn't see the mouthful of grease, cheese, and pizza I wolfed down..

'It's good right? Definitely one of my favorite investments for this place. To be honest with you, I thought this would save me the money of having to hire someone such as yourself.' He laughed, 'Turns out there are so many different ways people deal with stress. Food is just one of them.'

'Mr. Linguh, let me ask you something. I'm not one to sugar coat much and you seem pretty all right in my book, but what's up with you? Why do folks act like you are some boogey man?' I was feeling a little bold, and curious. I had already signed a contract, which was a binding agreement. What did I have to lose?

This guy really seemed to have quite the sense of humor, or at least find everything funny. He laughed again. Wiping his mouth, pretending to chew on his food for a moment. He leaned back in his chair and said, 'I'm the bad guy Lebannon. I take the fall for the stress that lands on some of these folks. Not everybody looks at me like that, but some find themselves in compromising positions once they become employed here. Some, not all, think I wasn't as honest as I could have been during the interview. We try to recruit more so than employ, but that isn't always sufficient. Due to the nature of the business, I have to be somewhat vague about things until contracts are in place and agreements are signed.'

He said that and it made me wonder what exactly could happen if an agreement was broken. Surely he couldn't just take people to court and share the nature of his business to an entire courtroom. Could the consequences be as sinister as the world the company ran to protect?

'I don't mind taking the blame. I don't mind that not everyone smiles at me in the hallways. There are a few that are more comfortable talking to me, but it's not that serious for me. My job is to ensure my business is run smoothly and that what the business is here for is successful. However people have to deal with their part, I've come to be okay with it. I even go any extra mile I can to ensure each and every employee is accommodated in those regards.'

'That's quite honorable of you Mr. Linguh. I must say I don't reckon I've met many employers who would take such care and consideration into the well being of the folks they have workin' for 'em.'

'I've learned over time that none of this works without the employees. It makes no sense for me to further treat them like shit when some of them are really struggling here. I understand that everyone has a line they'd like to think they won't cross, but I need people willing to cross that line for financial gain. I constantly need people to rotate in because not everyone can take it for a long period of time. And that's okay. To be frank, I may become a little concerned for those who can take it without much distress. Those seem more like the kind of folks that would be involved with what we are trying to monitor. That creates a bit of a conflict of interest.'

Mr. Linguh had long since finished the yogurt and fruit he had, now sipping on a bottle of water. I took the last bite of my pizza, wondering why they hadn't at least told me about THIS place before in the last two months. That was the best slice of pizza I had had in a very long time. The soda to go along with it was so cold and crisp. It was as if it bit my esophagus on the way down. All I could think of was wanting to try something else.

I figured at that point it would be rude to expect him to sit there with me as I taste tested and sampled things throughout the food court, so I decided I would go back when we were done with the tour.

We gathered the trash, wiped the table quickly, and headed back toward the corridor we came down. There were trashcans conveniently placed there so we dropped the trash off and kept walking.

'I'm going to show you the four other departments that are down here and then we will head off to your wing.' Mr. Linguh explained as we shuffled back down the light orange hallway we had come down. As the smell of food fainted into the background behind us, I could start to smell a fresh, sweet smell. I hadn't noticed it before, probably because I was so shocked all of this existed. It smelled almost like lavender maybe, a hint of vanilla. I wasn't sure, but it was quite pleasing. Almost calming. I instantly assumed that this was yet another measure Mr. Linguh had gone to ensure optimal stress relief throughout the facility.

I followed him to the left of the large room first. We walked down a long orange hallway this time. The color was deeper than that on the walls leading to the cafeteria. The walls had random abstract art all over them. From what I could tell, all the art pieces seemed to elicit a peaceful feeling, but I wasn't trying to think that hard about them. I was admiring what was happening around me, and eagerly waiting to see what was at the other end of the hall. In hindsight, I now realize that there was nothing done in that building that wasn't a subtlety of trying to lessen the stress of the work day.

'Down here is Department G,' he said as he badged into the doorway. 'All of these departments require badges to get in, if your security level isn't for that department, it won't allow you to come in. You, admin, and myself all have full access security to anywhere in the building, but other departments can't get in to their counter departments.'

Behind the door was a large, vaulted ceiling room. Inside, we were standing on a small balcony overlooking the entire room. There were stairs on either side of the small overlook to get down to the working floor.

There was calm and chaos all at the same time. Computer monitors were everywhere. There were some cubicles in the middle of the room, and other glassed in office-like cubicles toward the side. Every desk had at least four different monitors on it, along with a touch screen pad inside of the desktop. It was by far one of the techiest places I had ever witnessed in my life. To the right there was what looked to be some sort of snack bar, break room type area. It looked like a scaled down version of what I had seen in the cafeteria wing. There was a small seating area, a large refrigerator, a microwave, toaster oven, and small stations of premade food. Everything from pizza slices to bananas.

Seeing me looking in that direction, Mr. Linguh explained, 'Sometimes, they get pretty busy and don't have the time to get out to the cafeteria like they want, or maybe they just don't feel like walking out there. Fresh food and snacks are brought in every few hours or so to make sure if they need a snack or pick me up, they have it. Over there on the left are restrooms. The door all the way in the back is the back exit. All departments have their own doors that lead to a corresponding parking lot to make it easier for folks to get in and out without trucking around this whole facility.'

'So what do they do in here?' It didn't look very stressful, but I knew looks could be deceiving. It was almost as if he had read my mind.

'This is considered the least stressful of the four departments we will visit. They monitor the transactions of online goods. That sounds simple enough, but it's not so much. Anything that people want that they can't get by going to their local grocery or doctor, they can buy online. We've seen large transactions like houses, cars, boats, smaller transactions like prescription medicines, and everything in between.'

'I don't quite understand,' expressing my confusion. 'I don't see how that stuff is dark web or black market. Seems like typical consumer activity.'

'It is. It's more about the motive or means in which people obtain and/or purchase things that bring them to the dark web. For instance, let's say you have a house to sell; maybe there was something shady in the transaction or means of obtaining the house that keeps you from a realtor. Or you're addicted to pain meds; you can't just keep going to your doctor to fill pain med scripts, so you filter through the internet until you find what you need. Surprisingly, most of these transactions are online dealers. Not much going on that's real malicious, just illegal. This department deals with the overlying marketplace of the dark web, as you said the black market. Drugs, organs for transplants, etc.

You'll probably rarely, if ever, see any of these folks. They don't mind this job. It's one you kind of obtain by seniority, so they've all had their share of a separate department that is more stressful at some point or another. They either still need money, or actually like working for me for some odd reason.' He laughed at his own joke just as one of the employees walked past us on the floor. She smiled and waved. 'See, someone around here likes me,' he chuckled again as we left.

There we were, walking down that orange hallway again and all I could think to myself was, that wasn't bad at all. I mean not right, by legal standards, but not bad. So far, nothing I had seen made me understand why people were so stressed. Then I remembered he did say that was the least stressful of the four. It only got worse from there."

THIRTEEN

I let Lebannon sit there for a moment. I hadn't realized how hungry I was until he started talking about that food court. I was entangled in the story and curious to see where it went, but I was also suddenly starving. I didn't know what time lunch was. Of course, I didn't bring anything, which was foolish on my end.

Food and I have a nostalgically unhealthy relationship, so hearing about this grand cafeteria intrigued me. What more could I ask for? Suddenly in my mind I was considering how I would betray my own moral standing for a six-figure salary and as much free food as I wanted. Oh how quickly we can betray ourselves.

"I guess it's not that bad if some people still chose to work there long enough to be able to move to a different department," I said trying to distract myself from the oncoming hunger pains cramping my stomach.

"Well, that's debatable. From my experience, some people just have a higher tolerance for things than others. I don't know how long someone had to of worked their to be able to move to that department, but given my contract I'd only guess it wasn't as long as you probably think. Maybe a year or two at best."

"Well, Mr. Linguh sounds better than Chelsty made him out to be."

"I have to give it to you, you are absolutely correct about that. I honestly think that him being as open and honest with me helped me get through the time I stayed. We were actually pretty good friends I like to think. Until we weren't."

There was an awkward silence. I wasn't exactly sure what to say to that. We still hadn't quite made it that far along in the story. I was racking my brain trying to figure out what to say to get him to start talking again, without having to wait minutes and minutes until he snapped out of his daze.

"So what about the other departments, what were they like?" I don't know why it took me so long to find that question, but I was glad I found it. It got him right back talking, as if he had never stopped.

"The other departments got progressively worse. Next was what Mr. Linguh introduced as Department E. It was quite odd to say the least. Walking from one department to the other wasn't as quick as it sounds though. I mean yes they were all right there in that area, but quite frankly I don't believe I can fully explain to you how large that area actually was. It probably took a good four or five minutes to walk up the hall from Department G to get to the entrance of the hall to Department E.

That hall was a different shade, still orange, but moving closer to red. Let's say blood orange, which sounds reasonable I guess. I'm not a color connoisseur or nothin'. Anyway. We headed down that hallway, where Mr. Linguh warned me that now each department would get progressively more questionable.

Again he badged into the door at the end of the corridor and we stepped onto a small platform that over saw the rest of the room. This one was a little more involved than the last. The set up was essentially the same with a snack area, dedicated restrooms, and monitors everywhere. They had a few chalkboards that someone would run to and erase or add something to every few seconds.

'Welcome to Department E Lebannon. Here is where we monitor shall I say, odd purchases and fetishes.'

'Odd? Fetishes?' Those two words in relation to what we were looking at somehow made me just a little queasy. It was as if the grease from my pizza was suddenly throwing punches at the acid in my stomach.

THIRTEEN

'Yes. Well, there are more people than you'd care to know in the world that just aren't satisfied with the hand they've been dealt. Some people deal with that in normal, I guess you could say, healthy ways by societal standards. Others, however, flock to this side of the Internet to alleviate the pain, disappointment, or even envy they feel of others.

This is the area where people purchase, sometimes even trade, body parts mostly. For instance, let's say you aren't happy with your eyes. You see someone who had a better eye color than you. Well, there's a place, deep on the other side of the Internet where you can find real eyes that are the color you want and you can purchase said eyes, and someone to even transplant them for you...'"

"Why not just get contacts?!" I butted in horrified. I had never heard of such a foolish notion. I didn't want to judge too much, but how could people think that was the best way to deal with insecurity? *Were there people out there that really hated themselves that much they would go to such extremes?*

"Miss Ella, that was my exact question. I interrupted Mr. Linguh with that question in the exact same way you interrupted me. Kind of déjà vu'ish really. That was freaky." I smiled, watching him take over the deck of cards I had left laying on the table for some time. "He seemed amused by the question.

'Lebannon, you will quickly learn that rationale is not afforded to all. Some are so desperate and irrational that they resort to this.' He extended his hands, looking around the room. 'But it's not just body parts. There are chats and agreements for people to get in home cosmetic surgery, at a fraction of the cost you'd pay going into a clinic. There are even doctors, who have lost their credentials, that offer their services to suggest the appropriate cocktail of medications to create different illusions.

Like I said though, the body parts seem, for some reason, to be the most popular. At least for the last quarter.'

'Wait, you keep track of this stuff on a quarterly basis?'

'Yes, that is a portion of the job. Knowing what's in the highest demand allows us to ensure we create the ideal opportunities for these things to be obtained, and in turn increase rates accordingly.'

'Increase rates?' I didn't quite understand that part, so I asked as we headed back out to the long blood orange hallway and on to the next department.

'Oh yes, my apologies I haven't quite explained what helps pay that large salary I'm giving you.' There he was again purely amusing himself as he snickered along. 'You can't just get on the dark web and do whatever you want without giving something. It's imperative that we create a conducive atmosphere for all of these things to continue to progress. With that being said, a fee is involved to engage. Sellers and traders pay a certain rate, as do buyers. There are some who have what we deem as a membership, where they have paid a significant amount for all access. The particulars aren't that important because you won't have to handle that but yeah, we charge folks to use this service.'

That made complete sense. People would not just pay for their guilty pleasures; they would also pay significantly to indulge without fear of consequence or retaliation. I had to admit, it was genius for a business minded person. I knew these different industries on their own were lucrative, but putting them altogether and charging was beyond lucrative. It was the perfect storm.

While this being explained to me should have set off some sort of alarms within me, it made me more curious than anything. I should have realized then and there that Claire was probably right. Instead, my wheels were turning at the potential to increase my own finances. I should have realized something inside of me was slowly shifting, even then, but I didn't. It could have been my own pride getting in the way, not wanting to accept handouts. Maybe I was too arrogant to think these things couldn't affect me. I was nowhere near prepared for the task ahead of me. But I played the part like I did well.

THIRTEEN

We moved on to the next department. 'Now we're headed to Department W,' Mr. Linguh said.

The next corridor had lost most of the orange complexion and moved more towards red. This one, instead of art pieces had a pattern. There were swirls all over the wall in different shades of red, beautifully tangled together to create the illusion of texture. It was captivating to say the least. I honestly don't even remember what was on the walls to Department E. But what I do vividly remember was the odd hypnotizing affect of the swirl pattern down Department W's hall.

The set up was the same. Small overlooking balcony, cubicles and offices, break-room, restrooms, many monitors. This one however had a massive monitor in the middle of the room. There were actually two so you could see what was happening no matter what side of the room you were on.

'This is where things can start getting extremely stressful,' Mr. Linguh explained. 'In Department W, we monitor the selling, purchasing, trading, and auctioning of questionable goods. I say goods, but really most of this consists of potential victims, specifically for serial killers.' I was floored and my reaction was a dead giveaway. My mouth had opened up and I'm sure an audible gasp escaped that I was trying to hold in. For some reason, I had seemingly forgotten the terrible things Claire had shared with me. It was as if I really was hearing all the information for the first time. I guess being presented all those benefits had a way of covering up the sins, at least for a while.

Mr. Linguh patted the back of my shoulder, 'Yeah I know it's a lot to take in, but I told you what type of place this is. We benefit from staying in the trenches where people are willing to spend large sums of money on things we don't believe should be bartered.' He kept talking, as if it weren't odd at all. 'People have a lot of pinned up anger, frustration, and just overall sinister desires. Unfortunately for someone, that means there is always a market for people to be bought and sold for a killer's pleasures. This is the second highest paying department we have; we will be visiting Department L next, which is the highest paying.

There aren't just people bartered in this department though. We monitor the sales of weapons as well. Some of mass destruction, others of warfare; and everything in between. Then there are also poisons, mostly purchased to take care of insidious love affairs. Lastly there are hit men for hire. I'll tell you, when I first got started with all this, I thought this department would solely be hit men oriented. I was sorely mistaken. But they are still a part of the program. They just seem to have dwindled down drastically over the years. I guess people want to do their own dirty work these days.'

When we left that room, I realized there was a freshness that came over me walking past the threshold into the hypnotizing corridor. I hadn't paid it much attention, but the tension in Department W was so thick you could've cut it with a knife. Least that's what my Uncle Gene would've said. One more department to go and we were off to see where I would work. Finally. I felt like I had been at work longer that day than I had the entire two months prior. My workdays in the office were typically condensed to the morning, with just being on call in the evening.

I guess it didn't matter much. I didn't have anything else to do. Except I guess pack. I was given the address to my new condo as well as the keys and security code when I signed the documents with Mr. Linguh. He said I was free to move in at any time. I had been staying with a classmate whose parents paid his rent so I didn't have to further put myself in debt paying rent or for student housing. He was a party animal and never really there anyway, but I was kinda excited about having my own space. Come to think of it, it was going to be the first time in a very long time, if ever, that I was going to have my own place. I couldn't wait for the solidarity.

We headed to Department L. It had the most brilliant hallway of all. The red was blazing, such a magnificent color. The further down the

THIRTEEN

hallway you got though, the red transitioned into a tantilizing blue. As if it were a flame, starting at a normal burning temperature but changing color as the heat continued to rise.

All of the department wings were huge, but L was extraordinary. Instead of walking in onto a small overlooking balcony, we walked onto a balcony that surrounded the entire bottom floor. At the top were glassed in offices facing a monitor that covered an entire wall. There was a stairwell leading down to the work floor right beside the entrance, as well as across the room on the other side of the overlook.

Downstairs were two full wall monitors that mirrored the one at the top. There were dual cubicles throughout the room. With two designated restrooms it seemed to be the most spacious department. Even the break room was extraordinary. It was the closest to a full size cafeteria area as you could imagine. There was also a small dark room that seemed to have a couple couches, beds, and massage chairs.

'This is the department that brings in the most money. Over half of the total revenue actually. Being the most desired, it is the most stressful. There are a few extras in here to make every attempt to relieve stress. This is also the only department that works a rotating twelve-hour shift. I'm constantly trying to figure out the best way to work this department without burning out the employees I have here, but it requires so much manpower and unfortunately it has the highest turnover rate.' Mr. Linguh explained.

I hadn't paid much attention to what was on the monitors in any of the other departments, but something flashed across the huge monitor to my left that caught my attention. I didn't quite see what it was,. By the time I turned my head to look, it was gone. At the top of the monitor was what seemed to be a countdown calendar. There was a small box to the side with names and numbers. They changed so quickly I could barely make them out. The top line was in green. The number beside the name flashed frequently, but from what I could tell it was somewhere along the lines of $500,000. It was only going up from there.

There it was again. This time I got a good look. There was a picture of what appeared to be a young girl, no more than four or five. She was disheveled. Her hair was a curly mess on top of her head and her eyes were large and in pain. Jasmine. That was the name that flashed above her picture. Then the screen changed. It seemingly split into about ten different mini screens, all with the same type of information on them. Child after child, bid after bid, name after name ever changing on the board. It was a bidding war for these little children. And there were people out there, pedophiles no doubt, willing to pay upwards of a million dollars to have one.

Mr. Linguh didn't say anything for a moment. He stood there and let me take it all in. All the filthy and treacherous things that were flashing across the monitors. Probably not taking up a fraction of what the employees were really keeping track of.

Finally he spoke, starting towards the right walking around the overlook. I followed suit. 'As you can probably guess, this is the most immoral of the departments we have, hence why it is so stressful and holds the highest turnover rate. Here is where people pay to have their deepest, darkest, ugliest, and most reprehensible fantasies brought to life. It's the worst mainly because children and innocent women are involved. Most people have some capacity to understand the rage living in someone that would cause them to murder or torture. In the same way, most people don't have the capacity to understand an adult's desire in a child.

Nevertheless, here we monitor human trafficking, child pornography, and, as you can see, the bidding of available minors. We don't keep up with what people do with the things they purchase on the dark web. Granted, there are chats where like-minded people talk about different escapades and just share stories. It really isn't our business what happens after transactions. That's why we stay in business. We simply track and maintain the space for these folks to live out their most twisted nightmarish woes.'

THIRTEEN

We had walked around the top of the area, seemingly going unnoticed by those who diligently worked on the level below. They scurried about, sharing information with one another. I finally noticed they also had a number of white boards and chalkboards similar to Department W.

One young lady in particular who headed over to the break room caught my attention. I watched her grab a soda and some type of energy bar. She sat down, opened the bar and soda but never lifted them to her mouth. Everyone else walked around her and past her, but she just sat there with a blank look on her face. I was too far away to tell, but I felt like I could see the shimmer of a single tear fall down her cheek. As if that awakened her from her daze, she went back into work mode. Quickly eating the energy bar and drinking the soda, she grabbed another snack that I couldn't see and headed back to her workstation.

Even after we left Department L I could still see the dazed woman's face. It stuck with me. My mind kept showing me flashes of her blank stare across a background of monitors filled with innocent children. The woman was obviously stressed, but she also seemed to be doing whatever she could to get by. Yeah, I got all that just from watching her for a few minutes. She seemed like her life had taken a sudden wrong turn and she was going a direction that she didn't know how to navigate.

I wondered if that would be me. I wondered if I had just signed my conscious soul over for a six-figure salary and a little debt assistance. I remembered what my parents would say back when they were churchgoers, "The wolf can sometimes look like the sheep." Had I allowed the devil himself to sucker me into handing him my soul for a few months? I wasn't for certain. But I was curious to know how long that young woman had worked there, and how long had it taken her soul to completely drain?"

FOURTEEN

Heavy. That's what I felt as Lebannon drifted away into his place of recollection. Heavy and sad. I couldn't help but agree that what the owner said was right, everything up until Department L was somewhat understandable. I even found myself, after knowing how much money was on the table, justifying these horrible acts. Children though, they were just too innocent. Based on Lebannon's demeanor, I could only imagine it got worse. I really wasn't expecting the rest of his story, but I was definitely inclined to believe in his conspiracy theory.

The room was quiet again. The familiar rush of air from the vent swooshed past my ears. Then, much like the wind, it was gone. Nothing but a heavy silence, housing more thoughts and questions. I couldn't begin to recall how many times I completely forgot Ron was in the room. This was probably the longest pause in the story so far. Rightfully so. I didn't rack my brain trying to find the right things to say. I was aware enough of the trauma this was clearly bringing back that I just sat there for a moment. I say that as if it was for him, but it was really for me. I found my insides tense, quivering under the idea that there were innocent children, at that very moment, with their pictures and names flashing across a screen. Being bid on like they were antique artifacts.

The faint sound of birds chirping outside the window drew my attention. How different the world was depending on where you looked at it from. I watched as two beautiful birds seamlessly communicated with one another from either sides of the statue. Surely they had cares in the world, but they weren't these. They weren't these kind of cares and worries. No, these came only with the knowledge that the door of hell was wide open, sending evil to and fro amongst the crevices of the earth.

Evil had only been an abstract idea to me before meeting Lebannon. I had heard of it, maybe I had encountered it, but I wouldn't have known the difference. To me, most people were more so troubled, suffering from a trauma they hadn't quite learned to deal with. This though, this felt like evil. It felt like something so far from good, so beyond traumatic that it was scary. A chill went up the back of my neck, rolling from what seemd like my toes all the way up until it reached the nape of my hairline. My eyes rolled slightly, trying hard to see what suddenly entered the room. Not who, what. As we sat there in the heavy silence, my thoughts seemed to turn into demons right before my eyes. My stomach twisted and turned, over and over again. Bile tried to creep it's way up my esophagus and out of my mouth. It took everything in me to swallow it back down without drawing attention to myself. I seemed to be exposed again. This time, it was as if someone who appeared in a bright brilliance, only to lead me naked down a dark alley snatched off the blanket.

We didn't learn about evil in school. We learned about fears, traumas, delusions, and disorders. I had spent my entire college career learning of the things the human mind could accomplish. It was amazing really.

Now, at the end of my college career, I was faced with someone who had gone through the same studies I had, and was unprepared for the evil that awaited him. I dare say he was even hand picked by Satan himself.

Again, birds chirping shifted my focus. I hadn't even realized Lebannon had been trying to snap me out of my own disorganized daze.

"Ella, Ella, have I bored you that bad you have to ignore me now?"

"Huh? Oh, I'm sorry. What were you saying?"

FOURTEEN

He looked at me with a peculiar gaze, but didn't indulge where my mind had gone. "I suppose we've reached that point in the story that may help you better understand just how important my job was. More importantly why the knowledge I held was so sensitive as to land me in this palace." He glanced around the room.

"Mr. Linguh gave me a moment to gain my composure when we made it back to the middle of the large area that housed all the separate departments.

'Would you like to go back over to the cafeteria and grab a light soda or bottle of water? Maybe some crackers? I know this has been a lot to take in, but I would be leading you astray if I didn't warn you that going to your department next won't prove to be much better.'

He had a way of saying things bluntly, but with just enough care in his voice and gestures to make you think he really was worried and concerned about your well-being. I believed him, so we headed back over to the cafeteria to grab a quick snack and drink to settle the onset of nausea that I didn't know had swept over me. My knees knocked together as they poassed one another one foot in front of the other. They were trying to keep the weight of my body up despite them feeling like jello.

After a few minutes Mr. Linguh checked his watch saying, 'Let's get to it, shall we. Don't want to have to keep you too much longer before your first official day tomorrow.'

I followed him back up the stairs and out the door he originally badged in to. There was a door right outside to the left that I hadn't noticed before. A badge wasn't needed to get into it, but the door looked much older than everything else. It was as if it had been there years before the rest of the building. It was dingy, I couldn't tell if it had once been white or was purposely painted an off grey color.

We walked down a long hallway. It seemed to go on forever. Finally we came to a door. On the outside of the door was a chip to scan your badge. That was like all the other doors that required badging in to. This entryway, however, also had a small speaker on the outside of it with a button to push, no doubt to call in to whoever was on the opposite side.

Behind the door was a short hallway. It was kind of warm in there, much warmer than any other area of the facility we had visited so far. On the other side, was a door to the right. Right beside the door, oddly, there was a large, blue elevator. It was rustic, worn similar to the door that took us down the long journey to get here.

Mr. Linguh grabbed the handle to the door beside the elevator, 'This will be your office.'

I was confused. I remembered Claire sharing with me that I wouldn't be doing what I had been doing during internship, but there was no one else on this end of the facility. Walking into what Mr. Linguh described as my office made matters a little more confusing for me.

Behind the door was a large room, much larger than I expected. It wasn't the room itself that surprised me, however. A large desk was at the far end of the office. On the desk were a few monitors, some of which seemed to look like a security system. On the right side of the desktop was a touch screen, built in pad, like I had seen in the other departments. On the left side was what looked like a control panel. Filing cabinets and shelving units surrounded the desk. On the right side was a set up similar to that of the other departments. I didn't have a dedicated break-room, as I could only assume I was literally going to be the only person working in the room. There was a restroom, a snack section, and a small room with a two-chair set up; that was somewhat like the way the chairs were set in the office I had been using for the past few months. They were across from one another, one a large high backed chair, the other more of a chaise. There were two small side tables, and a purified water container.

That all sounds fine and dandy, right? Yeah that's not what confused me about this office. On the left, what you thought would have been another wall. Instead, there was a two-way mirror that covered the entire span of the room. I could even see down to what I could only

FOURTEEN

assume was the first floor. It was the inside of the elevator next to the door. The inside however, didn't look like anything I had ever seen. Yes, it looked like a typical elevator, but it seemed…."

"Seemed what?" I asked as he trailed off, unsure of what the right word to say was.

"Scorched. As if it had been in a fire."

"Scorched?" I didn't think I had heard that right.

"Yeah Miss Ella, scorched. The inside of the elevator was dark and rusty. It seemed to be filled with burn marks on the walls and was covered in what I soon found to be soot."

I gave Lebannon a moment to gather himself. I had apparently stopped breathing because my body suddenly gasped for air. He let out a huge sigh and went on. "Mr. Linguh gestured towards the small seating area and asked me to have a seat so he could explain what the expectations of me really were. He took a moment, not sure if it was for genuine pause to formulate the words or if it was just a dramatic affect to make me think he was concerned by whatever my reaction would be.

'Lebannon, this is what you're job is going to be,' he said in one breath.

I looked around; confusion contouring my face into twists and turns that felt unnatural. 'What exactly IS my job Mr. Linguh?'

'As you've seen, and experienced to an extent, there are aspects of this job that are extremely stressful. As I've also explained to you during this tour, I have gone to great lengths to make sure there is a plausible outlet for everyone to relieve their stress.' He leaned back in his chair, which I came to realize was a tell that he was about to go into more detail about something. 'I've learned many different methods of dealing with that over the years, as I'm sure you've seen today. This is one of the methods that I did not come to lightly, however it became evident that it was a necessary outlet. Through that two way mirror is an elevator. I'm sure you saw the elevator door as we came in. That, Lebannon,' he gestured towards the mirror where I could see the inside of the elevator. Even from across the room I could see the scorched marks climbing up the walls. 'That's our suicide elevator. And you are going to be overseeing and assisting those employees who choose to use it.'"

FIFTEEN

"A what?" I couldn't see my own face, but I felt my eyes grow wide. As if I strained them, the corners of my eyes pulled in a small tear of pain. My eyebrow seemed to reach the top of my forehead. I startled myself, jumping as the question flew out of my mouth. I was louder than either of us had been in a while. I even thought I saw Ron jumo slightly out of the corner of my eye.

Of all the things I was expecting him to say, suicide elevator was nowhere near the list. It wasn't even something I could have considered. What kind of job was this? Why would they encourage suicide? I mean, if I go back and remember that the nature of this job does consist of people allowing the most degrading and inhumane things to happen with no consequence. They literally made their living ensuring no repercussions came to these people who helped keep the lights on and the salaries paid.

It was easy for me to sit there and judge in that moment, but it wasn't my story. It wasn't my place to judge what was happening. I still didn't have all the facts, and it wasn't about how the stories made me feel. It was about how these things affecting Lebannon, and more importantly what happened to land him in an insane asylum, cut off from the rest of the world. Even still, we had long since moved past flirtatious gestures and gone down a rabbit hole of darkness. I was starting to lose sight of the light.

He ignored my question. I can't blame him. It was pretty rhetorical anyway. He continued, "I didn't think I heard him correctly. I stared at him with a blank look on my face.

'I didn't come to the decision lightly,' he continued, ignoring the confusion and horror protruding through my facial muscles. 'I always encourage employees to share their tips and input with me. I forgot to point out the suggestion boxes throughout the facility, but this was actually a highly requested suggestion.

That elevator only opens beside your door. If an employee feels that what they've seen or experienced is beyond their ability to carry on, or they have just reached their limit, we provide a safe space for them to end their own life. This allows employees to always know they are supported and that their decisions matter to us. It also helps to ensure that there aren't many questions asked or fingers being pointed in the event of a police presence.

Most employees that reach this point have either pushed their loved ones away, or present an elaborate plan to ensure no one comes looking for them. They don't really leave suicide notes, though some have in the past. We don't have any requirements as far as that is concerned, though again we don't want to have the police snooping around.'

As he said this, all I could think of was Hubert. Had he come here? Was his sudden fling and desire to escape his wife with a new love interest a part of his elaborate lie to cover his own suicide? It made sense, and yet I had not seen it coming. There was an empty feeling in the pit of my stomach, slowly being filled with dread. Emotions I didn't even know I could feel poured into that pit, only to be regurgitated to me soul. I wished Claire had told me all of this. What she said was minor compared to what I was being faced with in that moment. I couldn't even bring myself to think about her other than that. It was the only hope I could think of to help handle the churning pit of emotions that had taken over my stomach. But it was no hope at all. Not then anyway.

FIFTEEN

'Okay...' Anxiety welled up inside of me, taking over my fingers as they fidgeted with the buttons on my shirt. All the confidence I had just hours earlier as I was trying to pull information out of him had forsaken me. I was now faced with the harsh reality of what I had just signed up for: Hell. 'So, how exactly does this work? And what is it that I'll be doing?'

I got up and walked toward the mirror, staring into the bare elevator. Mr. Linguh didn't get up behind me. He simply turned slightly in his chair, but left me to my own observations.

'Well, you'll still see employees from time to time, but it will be less face time than what you have gotten used to. For those employees, your communication will stick to emails, chats, and a few phone calls here and there. When employees want to come specifically to get in the elevator, a request will be made that goes directly into a system you have access to.

Upon arrival, said employee expresses their intent. Once you have verified multiple times this is truly what they want, they get inside the elevator.' He shifted suddenly, getting up from his chair to join me in front of the mirror. 'This is a one-way mirror, as you've probably deduced. You will always be able to see inside, but they won't be able to see you once they enter. When they are ready, they push the button to go to level 1. The elevator automatically start, along with a fire.'

'A fire?!' I was practically yelling the question. It didn't seem to phase him though.

'Yes. The elevator incinerates those who enter it. From the time it takes the elevator to go down to the first floor, where the doors obviously never open, and come back up, the elevator is totally consumed in flames. Typically, that is all the time that it takes for someone to become fully incinerated.'

I'm not sure if Mr. Linguh ignored it, or didn't see the tear that ran down my face. It was warm and stung as it slowly rolled over my cheek down to my chin. The trail eventually dried, leaving behind an itchy line. What had I gotten myself into? I tried desperately in that moment to bring all of the benefits to the forefront of my brain. No matter how hard I tried though, I couldn't find them. It was as if they were hiding behind all of the things I had seen and heard in the last hour.

I never was one to be emotional. I don't really have much empathy either. That may sound harsh, but it's not something everyone carries ya know. In that moment though, staring into that dark elevator, all I could think of was watching people burn to death. All I could hear was screams of people being burned alive. All I could smell was that of burning flesh. I was no longer standing there in front of an elevator in my office. My body was there, yes, but my mind had taken me to a flaing arena surrounded by various scorched bodies. It was only when Mr. Linguh spoke again that I was jolted back to reality from the hellish daydream that had consumed me.

'There isn't a panic button, or a way to stop the elevator once it has been activated. Every employee has full understanding that this option can't be undone. That's why it's important for you to check, double check, and triple verify that anyone who comes here to see you is absolutely sure that's what they want to do. We haven't implemented anything other than the incinerator yet, which means unfortunately any poor soul that chooses this as their stress relief goes in alive. They have to activate the elevator themselves; it has to be their choice all the way to the end.'

He pulled away from in front of the mirror before I did, walking towards the other end of the room where the desk set up was.

'A cafeteria runner will also bring you fresh food a few times throughout the workday for your snack area. There are records in these filing cabinets of each employee with a history of extreme distress or mental breakdown throughout the workday. These buttons control the elevator, and by control I mean in the event that someone isn't fully incinerated during the first ride, you have to send them back through again. There is also an intercom system where you will buzz employees

FIFTEEN

in who come to see you, and it is also linked to the inside of the elevator where you can talk them through it should you see fit.

Your work schedule is somewhat similar to what you had before. You're really only REQUIRED to be here when you have someone coming here to see you. We've set it up that appointments are made in advance, to allow employees time to change their mind should they desire. You'll know your load at least one day before. Sometimes there are situations that come up that may be deemed emergency, which is why you will always be on call. That is quite rare though. There are a few administrative tasks that need to be done to document any and all interaction you have with employees. That will probably take up a decent amount of your day, but you should still be able to head off campus at a nice time.'

Mr. Linguh rattled all this off as if he was speed racing to teach me everything I needed to know in the next minute. I wasn;t even sure he had taken a breath. He stopped abruptly. I could only assume it was to let me take it all in. Maybe it was finally to breathe. I was still standing in the same spot, eyes glued to the mirror in front of me. My eyes were fixated on a specific section of soot in the corner of the elevator. Down at the bottom. It was caked on, like there was just ash on top of ash that covered and burned into the corner. The more I stared at it, the more alive each piece of ash seemed to be. I was faced with the only remembrance of people being the impression of ash they made in the corner of that elevator. Was Hubert the freshest of the pile?

I didn't know for sure, but I assumed I'd probably figure out when I started the next day. There was no going back. The contract was signed. I had heard Mr. Linguh explaining some of the duties and the scheduling expectations, but it just went in my ears. His words were garbled, running around in the free spaces of my head. All of my attention, the forefront of my mind, was on that spot in the corner. It was as if the souls of everyone who had entered the elevator were all cryin' out at me at the same time. I had never felt such a thing, and never wanted to feel it again."

"It felt like an eternity from the time Mr. Linguh left me alone in that office to when I finally decided to leave. At some point he explained where the exit was to my small personal parking lot for easier access to my new office. Shortly after he looked at his watch, took a deep breath, and let me know he had a meeting to attend. I was done for the day and free to go. He made sure I had the keys to my new condo and knew what time to show up the next day. He walked toward the door but stopped behind me, placing his hand on my shoulder. After a moment he left, leaving me to stare at the corner of the elevator all by myself. I don't think I said anything. I just stood there, staring at all the souls piled into that small corner.

My walk was slower than normal, almost depressed. I slumped deeper and deeper with each step on my way around the building to where I was arked. I knew I was going to have to snap out of it soon, but I just wanted to embrace it for a moment.

I should have gone the long way through the inside of my facility to stop by Claire's desk. But I didn't have it in me. One thing for sure, having a dedicated entryway that would eliminate human interaction was perfect. I didn't quite feel like being bothered. I knew she understood though, I checked my phone once I fell into the driver's seat.

Hope you're not too freaked. Tried to warn you. Call me later

I don't think I even turned the radio on. I just drove, in silence. My tires rolled effortlessly across the roads, only letting off a small sound with each tiny split of concrete it crossed. When I finally pulled up in front of my place, I sat there, trying hard to focus on the hum of the engine. I just didn't have it in me to move. I knew that no one was home, but sitting there in my car just seemed better. The engine purred ever so lightly underneath the hood. The more I focused on it, the calmer the

FIFTEEN

blistering pit of emotions seemed to become. A scream at a neighboring house shook me, thrusting me back to reality where my heart rate increased at the sudden loud noise.

I let out a loud sigh, pulling out my phone. I had saved the address to the new condo. Clicking on the address I checked the map, realizing it wasn't too far away. I couldn't stay in that funk forever. I had the next six months to get through, and all of a sudden I realized I was probably going to see way worse than I ever thought.

I didn't have much really. Clothes, shoes, laptop, and some other items. It didn't take long to pack everything I owned into my car. I wrote a quick note letting my roommate know I had found a place, for whenever he came back."

"You just moved into that condo? After seeing what they were going to have you do?" I didn't plan on interrupting him, but the shock weled up inside of me taking over my voice box. I didn't understand why he still went ahead with the job. I still didn't even understand how that job existed.

"Why not? They were still giving it to me; I was still going to have to fulfill my contract. The way I figured it, if I was about to put myself through hell for six months just to get ahead, I might as well milk every cow they put in front of me. It didn't make right good sense to not take advantage of this place when everything was going to be fully paid for, even after I graduated.

It took a minute to shake what I was feeling. But if I must admit, it didn't take as long as I felt like it should. I focused my energy during the drive on imagining what a new place would be like.

It wasn't at all like I expected. When I thought of a condo, I figured it would be a building with plenty of other folks ya know. Like some fancy apartment building. It wasn't like that. There were other condos, but the whole building probably had 10 folks living there in all. There was a doorman who let me in. I introduced myself and he showed me the way to my spot. The look of pity he gave me let me know he knew exactly what I had been tasked. I followed him, wondering how many folks in that city were in Mr. Linguh's pockets? Even more interestin' was how he managed to keep everyone quiet.

For a split second, I forgot all the baggage that came with my new place. It was huge, and beautiful. I hadn't ever been in a place so nice; don't even recall having friends with anything remotely close to this. Even the suite I shared with my classmate thanks to his rich parents didn't compare. It was, indeed, fully furnished. I can only assume for my convenience the fridge and pantry was fully stocked too. Mr. Linguh must have also had an interior decorator in his back pocket, because it looked like something in a home décor magazine. My taste definitely wasn't that fancy.

The door attendant, Jinx, explained that he could always be reached. Apparently I had access to somewhat of a personal assistant in him. Whatever I needed, I could just let him know and he would have it delivered for me. It was like having all access room service. I thanked him and he left me to bask in the wealth status I suddenly had. I coulda only imagined had Momma and I's relationship stayed on good terms, I probably woulda been inclined to tell her how I was livin'. Even if it was temporary."

His country twang got worse for a second, but I kept up. I wondered if he had spent time trying to minimize the weight of his accent around people. Maybe that was why sometimes he was more understandable than others.

"It only took me about two trips, maybe three, to get all my things in the condo. Like I said, it's not like I was packed heavy. I didn't have much. I set up my workspace, quickly hung my clothes, and headed to the kitchen. There was pretty much anything I could have wanted. I started to grab a soda but paused noticing the cans of beer. I grabbed one of them instead. I popped the can open, almost startling myself. I had forgotten how much force I could put into things sometimes, as loud as that can popped was proof of that., I just stood there for a minute. I was stuck. I couldn't move. I was standing in the middle of a beautiful condo with

FIFTEEN

a beer in my hand physically. Mentally though, behind my eyes, I was starin' at a corner filled with ashes. That was all I could see.

That trance held me hostage for probably fifteen minutes before I chugged the rest of the beer in the can, smashing it on the countertop when I was done. A small victory celebration erupted in my head at the idea of having a place where I could smash cans on the counter whenever I wanted. Not to mention chugging beers.

I told myself to shake everything off, literally. I walked around the island shimmying my shoulders and arms, allowing my hands to flail lifelessly as they smacked the opposite sides of my body. I really wanted to call Claire, but I had to figure things out first. I decided to text her. The message she had sent was still there on my phone; I had never responded.

Call you in a bit. Don't fall asleep.

It was a high school thing to say. Why would a grown woman choose to stay up and wait for a call? But it was all I had. That was when I realized just how much time in the day I had lost. It seemed as if only a few hours had passed since I left the office, but when I checked the time it was almost eleven. I had to pull myself together and come up with some way to get through it all. The idea of losing time seemed like a viable option, at least for the next six months. But I knew well enough that that could cause more problems than I'd probably want.

Six months. That's what I kept tellin myself. It was only six months, I could do this. There were plenty of folks in the world who committed suicide on a daily basis and I was no more different because of them. I told myself it was my job, no more no less. I didn't know these folks, and would ensure that I didn't take any steps towards getting to know them either. I would go in to work, oversee, and mind my own business. Whatever that meant.

By the time I called Claire back it was almost midnight. We came to an agreement that we wouldn't talk about work. Just us, or the weather, or anything other than work. I wasn't that familiar with her yet, so I didn't want to share the dark places my mind had to visit just to ensure I got through the upcoming months. I was surprised she was so understanding though. I guess it just came with her knowing how dark what I would have to deal with really was.

I loved talking to her. She definitely took my mind off everything, all of my attention was on her. Maybe I could use her as my crutch. It was a lot of pressure to put on her; pressure she wouldn't even know was being exerted. It was selfish really, manipulative even. At that point, though, I realized that if I was going to make it through the next six months, I was going to have to do whatever worked. Didn't matter how selfish or unreasonable it was.

That's the reality I went to bed with that night. As soon as Claire's voice was no longer contributing to the vibrations of my eardrums, it was right back to that ash stained corner. Right back to the trance. I didn't have nightmares that night like I thought I would. Instead, once I was sleeping, everything seemed calm. Almost serene. Yes, there was a small haunting in the back of my mind of the impending dread that was now my responsibility. It was as if it were a thorn, ever so small at the base of my brain. But my dreams, my dreams that night were filled with financial success. My dreams brought reassurance with receipts from loan payments, a savings account beyond my wildest dreams, stocks and options. My dreams reminded me that if I kept myself together for the next six months, I really didn't have to do much else the rest of my life if I played my cards right. Some could say that meant I wasted my time getting a degree, but not really.

Had I not ended up in Mr. Riley's class, I would have missed out on the opportunity, if you could call it that. Sure, my mental health probably would have been better off, but my pockets would thank me. My dreams reminded me that in six short months, my life would be set. I just had to make it to the end. Some may have attributed such positive reassuring dreams to their God. I, on the other hand, knew it was probably Satan trying to encourage me to believe signing my life away was no big deal.

At that, my alarm blasted. I had woken up in a new place, almost forgetting where I was. It was the first day of a long sentence in hell."

SIXTEEN

Things were getting interesting. Very interesting. Lebannon got up abruptly, starting me. My eyes grew wide and a small yelp escaped my mouth. I wasn't expecting such a sudden movement. He walked across the room where Ron was, catatonic. I had completely forgot he was there. I realized it was the first time I got to see Lebannon's full stature. He was toned well, stronger than I would have thought him to be. He was also shorter than I expected. He seemed to tower over me if he was sitting upright in front of me, but he couldn't have been much taller than me from head to toe. His torso was longer than average, giving the illusion he was taller than he really was if he was sitting down.

His walk was just as mysterious as he first appeared to be. It was quite dapper if I must admit. There was a part of me, deep down, a part of me that I don't even want to admit I met. That part of me, in the faintest of long shots was dare I say; attracted to him. Living arrangements aside, he was quite the catch. I had yet to find an inkling or reason for him to have been locked away with the insane for so long. Sure, there were things that he admitted to that were dark and a little twisted, but there I was semi attracted to him despite that. Didn't make him any more insane than I was, right?

I stayed still, following him with my eyes. He leaned down towards Ron, saying something that I couldn't hear. I watched him carefully move him from in front of the tv, back to the seat by the wall he was at when I first arrived. He was caring, almost fatherly with Ron. I didn't quite understand it, but somehow it touched me.

"These folk needa start givin' me some of their checks the way I tend to thangs round here," he said as he approached the table we were sitting at. His twang was back in full affect. I could tell he was trying to minimize the gesture he had just done with Ron, so I didn't push it. "They always forget to come move ole Ron about from time to time. Probably somewhere with their heads up their... Oh never mind! Where was I?"

"You're first day in hell," I said smiling, I'm sure to him it probably was torturous, but describing it as hell was a bit of a far fetch. It amused me, though it was somewhat at his expense. Luckily, he had a sense of humor.

"Ahh yes, hell was quite the place." I wasn't sure why he had to say it in a random British accent, but it made it funny nonetheless. "My first day wasn't so bad. I had to get used to the new scenery and being so far away from others in the building. I was used to being able to walk out of my office and see other people, that wasn't really the case here.

There were a few more administrative tasks to take care of when I got in. By administrative, I mean there was another stack of paperwork waiting on my desk for me to sign. I didn't really bother reading most of it. I skimmed through, signed, and moved on to the next. I tried for a while to refrain as much as possible from looking past the mirror to the inside of the elevator. I quickly realized that the more I wanted to make myself not look, the more inclined I was to look. Finally I got over it and told myself it was a part of what I would have to deal with, so the quicker I got used to it the better. It didn't really bother me much after that.

The first day gave me the hope that the day before had snatched away. I spun around in my chair for a while as if I were a child before finally logging in to the computer. It started dinging non-stop with emails. I went through them one by one, filtering what was important

SIXTEEN

and what wasn't. I figured the one from Mr. Linguh was probably important so I opened it up.

Lebannon,

It's so great to have you on the team! I am very pleased that you accepted my offer and hope it is beyond your expectation. I have attached a few simple training videos to familiarize yourself with how the controls work to the elevator. There is also a document of instruction on how to get into the company portal and chat where you can see everything that goes on. That is where a lot of your communication will take place. The security cameras should have unlocked automatically upon logging in at this workstation.

Included in the training material is an explanation of some of the new icons you may be unfamiliar with on your desktop, such as the FoodMe App.

I have contacted Mr. Riley who has taken the necessary steps to excuse all of your future classes in order for you to focus on work. He will be sending you information on your graduation and attending options.

Finally, I have attached a list of the benefits afforded to you for your record, to include pension options and future contract terms.

Feel free to message or email me if you need anything

Sincerely,

Mr. Linguh

 There were so many documents attached to that email, and I didn't really feel like sorting through them. I opened up the two I was most curious about, the app explanations and the benefits. The FoodMe App was apparently the program used by the cafeteria. I could place an order for anything I wanted, or even request certain snacks be stocked in my office on certain days. It was quite fancy, almost too fancy for an ole countryman like myself. I remember ordering steak and eggs to start the day as I planned to progress through learning all of the new apps and systems. I messed around in some of the apps for a while, then pulled up the company system.

I was shocked, and intrigued. I could see everything. From the stats in Department E to the bids and auctions taking place in Department L. Even the cameras around Claire and Chelsty's office areas. I had full access to each department and everything that was no doubt on their computer screens; I had the ability to see on mine. Not personal stuff though, just the shared stuff like on the big screens. I wasn't quite sure if that was going to make thing easier or more complicated. One thing I did figure, it would definitely pass a little bit of time.

Finally, I pulled up the document label "Benefits." It was all the same stuff he had told me when he offered me the position, just in writing. I scrolled to the last few pages to "Pensions and Future Contract Options." I apparently had the opportunity to know what the options were after my contract was up, even now. I was so sure that I would just do it until the six-month mark, make the money then never look back. The figures at the end of that document however, appealed to a different part of me.

After my six-month contract was up, I had options to re-sign anywhere from one to another six months. At that point, the salary ranged from $24,000 for an additional month to $200,000 for an additional six months. The amounts nearly doubled for every contract signed after that. The document went on to explain that in the event I was employed by the company for a total of 24 months, I'd be eligible for $750,000 a year for thirty years. That would be the automatic pay rate for anytime I chose to work after the 24th month, or if I didn't chose to work at all.

Those numbers took me back to the dreams taking over my mind the night before. Those were figures I had never even dreamed of. I was never trying to reach those kind of numbers. Surely, you can relate to that. If I was planning to make that much money I definitely wouldn't have chosen the field that had miraculously, or should I say devilishly landed me in that predicament. But it had. From that moment on my

SIXTEEN

mind always considered those numbers. Oh, the thangs I could do with those numbers. I reckon that was a point when my morality further took a back seat. It may have even slipped out the back exit door before I knew it."

He trailed off for a moment thinking about it. I sat there, allowing my mind to think on what that kind of money would mean for me. What would I do? Would it be worth my own mental health? People always talked about money not being able to buy happiness, was this one of those instances? I really couldn't imagine having access to that much money. He was right, if I thought about networthing anything close to that, I'd have picked a different degree field.

"The first few months weren't that bad. Really. I started to think that it was the fear of the unknown that made things so difficult for me in the beginning. For the amount of money they were paying, I anticipated I would be watching people fry by the dozens. It wasn't like that though. I spent most of the day chatting with employees concerning their immediate stress levels. It was similar to what I was doing before, just through a computer. Sometimes I had chats miles long with employees. Other times it was short, sweet, and to the point.

Things with Claire were escalating. She had even spent the night with me a few times. She loved the condo, but I had a strange feeling that she knew a little more about it than she should. It was as if she had been there before.

It took a couple weeks before the first person came to the elevator. Her name was Xenna. We had chatted a few times, but she was one of the short thread ones. I got the notification and I can't lie to ya, my heart sank a little bit. I hadn't really been prepared for it. I had been spoiled by the lack of interest in that part of my job. No one, before her, even inquired about it.

Shortly after I was made aware, Mr. Linguh chatted me:

I'll attend the first one with you.

I guess that was comforting, a little. I was back to the fear of the unknown. I had to tell myself over and over again that everything would be fine. But I wasn't confident or sure of that at all. I picked my phone up from the small cutout section of my desk and texted Claire:

Stay with me tonight. Need to see you.

Okay baby, be there around 8. Chinese?

That's fine.

Tossing my phone back into it's cut out I opened the document labeled "Elevator Instructions Manual." Since I hadn't needed the information so far, I never bothered to open it. The day had finally come though, and I didn't want to make things any worse by not knowing what to do if I needed to. Especially in front of Mr. Linguh. The words were there, the buttons were there, but it took about an hour for me to comprehend what I was looking at. It wasn't because the document was difficult to read, or even that the buttons were improperly labeled. My mind just couldn't sit still long enough for me to retain what I needed to know. Somehow, I had gotten locked back into that trance in my mind. I was pulled back into that flaming room staring at all the souls that housed themselves one on top of the other. A pile of ashes in a corner, waiting for the next soul to join.

I got up and went into my own personal snack pantry and grabbed a soda. It had never occurred to me to drink while I was on the clock. The desire never fluttered past my mind, until then. What the heck, right? This wasn't even a normal job with normal standards. Sitting back down at the desk I checked the FoodMe App out of curiosity and sure enough I could request beer, wine, and hard liquor to be stocked for me. Whatever my taste of juke juice was, it was at my disposal."

"Juke juice?" That was a new one to me. I clearly wasn't from the same kind of south he was.

SIXTEEN

"That's what Momma started calling anything that made her slutty. Kinda picked it up along the way."

"Very well."

"Anyways, I put in a few requests and back to the document I went. For the first time, I noticed the instructions indicated it was okay for me to operate the elevator for practice purposes, as long as no one was in it without consent. What the hell? That's what I thought. I'm already here, might as well go for it. I took a long, hard gulp of soda. It was ice cold and kicked the back of my throat like a toddler who just learned karate. After a long ahhhh, I set to it. I followed all the instructions and read, then reread all of the functions of each button. Once I felt confident, I fired it up. Literally.

All of a sudden, there was a brilliant blaze behind the mirror to my left. My eyes stared in a combination of horror and amazement. I seemed to elevate from my chair across the room to the one-way mirror. It was like something out of a cartoon. Least that's how I remember it. My eyes grew wider by the second as the flames seemed to engulf the entire elevator shaft, top to bottom. I couldn't help but imagining Hubert willingly stepping in, pushing the button to his fiery demise.

The shaft was consumed, but I couldn't quite see any smoke. I wasn't sure if the flames were just that bright, or if maybe there was some vent to filter the smoke like they had at the fancy steakhouses. Through the flames, I watched as the elevator lowered to the bottom floor, sat there for a few seconds, then climbed back up to rest at it's start position. I hadn't even realized the elevator actually made dingin' noises at each floor. About ten seconds after the second ding, indicating it had made it back to the top, the flames vanished in a brilliant flash. As if they were an atomic explosion being sucked back into the earth. Just like that, they were gone.

I breathed for the first time in two minutes. My lungs suddenly gasping, grabbing at the oxygen I had been depriving myself of unconsciously. If I didn't think about the fact that a person would be inside of that the next day, it really was quite fulgurating. Amazing even. The design work on somethin' like that was impeccable really. The fire consumed the elevator, but it didn't burn up. There was a teeny tiny little remembrance of a boy inside me. That boy might relate it to a Bible story some Sunday school teacher taught me. Long before I was thrown into the fiery furnace of the world leaving those teachings to rot in a lonely filing cabinet of rust in my mind.

A single tear escaped yet again. The first time it happened, in that very spot, I thought it was because I really was moral. It was because I was terrified of the reality staring back at me from inside the empty, dense elevator. This time though, without the presence of Mr. Linguh, this time was different. This time was me realizing I was admiring the beauty of a creation designed to execute. This tear was the acknowledgement of my mind that something lived deep enough in my soul to have gotten me that far, and dark enough to make this job work for me.

A red flash inside the elevator accompanied by a buzzin' alert bought me back to reality. It was reminding me to either restart the elevator to finish something unfinished, or power it down. I can't lie to ya Ella, ya know I was bout tempted to do one more run through, just to see if it was going to be the same. But, I decided against it. I sat down at my desk, watching the chats fill up with people desperate for someone to share their frustration with.

I took another swig of the soda I had gulped down a few minutes before. It was crazy how so quickly the fizz died down to a small bite in the back of my throat compared to the karate kick I had gotten earlier. I cracked my knuckles, pushed the thoughts of blazing fires to the back of my mind and started typing away."

The effortless switch from proper and educated, to twangy and broken English was odd. I clearly knew his was educated, and I always chose to believe in someone being able to be intellectually capable without having to sound the part. I wondered again if he was doing it to impress me, or if he found more enunciation better for me to follow

SIXTEEN

along. I didn't think I was the type of person that really had to code switch much around people, but I had plenty of friends who did. Then again, I guess everyone code switched from time to time. Professional verses how I talk with friends. Either way, I hadn't ever really heard anyone do it so frequently while talking to the same person. It was almost as if he forgot he was playing a role from time to time.

I was overthinking. That's what I told myself. It had to be his emotions or something that was triggered by certain parts of his story. Either way, though it was odd I had long since forgotten my secret agenda to diagnose him. So even if it was a potential indicator of something, I missed it completely.

He went on for a moment about his night with Claire, but I tuned out for a moment. Something he said made me realize that the more I followed along with his story, the more I found myself justifying his decisions. I justified his desire to accept the contract against all moral acceptances because in my mind, at that time, I started to feel like I would do it too. He had a way of making me feel almost sorry for him. More than that, he had an uncanny ability to draw you in to his point of view. Subtly pushing his perspective on you, no matter what angle you looked at it from. The longer I listened, the more I started to believe that he was faced with impeccable opportunities and deep down he would have been a fool not to take them. That had me questioning my own moral compass.

"Ella, did I bore you again?"

SEVENTEEN

"I'm sorry, what?" If I kept spacing out he was going to think I was uninterested in what he had to say. That wasn't the case at all though. I was being prompted with everything he said to do more self-reflection than I cared to admit. It was the kind of self-reflection that I couldn't seem to put off until later. It just happened. He would say something, then do one of his long dramatic pauses and down the rabbit hole of my mind I would go. "No, no. Go ahead."

"Pleasure to have your permission," the sudden swooshing sound of air flowing through the cards as he shuffled them filled the room. "I was so nervous the next day. I was nervous because again, the unknown is awful. I had saw the flame and knew what to expect there. It wouldn't be the complete first time I watched the elevator in action. What was unpredictable: Xenna. I didn't know what to expect from her, nor did I know what types of emotions would come with watching someone take their life in front of me. I thought maybe I could just focus on the flame like I had during the practice run, ignoring the fact that someone was in the elevator altogether.

I kissed Claire on the forehead. She was still sound asleep in bed. I needed to leave a little earlier than she had to get up. I fixed up a quick breakfast, made a pot of coffee, and left a note on the counter letting her know I had an early appointment at work. While she had been staying at my house frequently, we weren't so advanced that she needed a key. I had just gotten to have a little privacy and space to myself. I didn't mind sharing it with her, but we didn't need to share it so much that she needed a key.

Luckily, the fancy place Mr. Linguh had put me up in had Jinx. I let Jinx know that Claire was still sleeping and asked if he would lock up when she left. Ain't that ironic? I didn't want the girl I was sleepin' with to have a key, even if it was just to lock up after a night of raunchy escapades; but I was perfectly fine with a man whom I ain't know from Adam going to lock up once she left.

Surprisingly, Mr. Linguh was waiting for me in my office when I got in. 'It's a big day for you, the first time you have to use the elevator. We had a pretty long stint there where no one needed to use it. Happens like that sometimes. Stress can be unpredictable and you never really know how often people are going to choose certain stress relief options.'

He was sitting at one of the chairs in the small seating area. He was doing something with his phone and barely looked at me as he said all of that. He didn't bother to get up, and I wasn't in the mood to extend pleasantries.

'Well, I guess the day has come indeed.' I headed to my desk, pulling out Xenna's file.

'I'll be here more so for support for you, since it's your first time and all. Want to ensure it runs smoothly and that you have a live person to ask questions should you need. Can't quite trust these computers with that sort of thing, not in this specific capacity. You follow through the protocol you've read up on and I'll be right here.'

'Sounds good.' Xenna was supposed to be there in about fifteen minutes. It was just enough time for me to gather all the documents that we needed her to sign. M eyes fumbled around as I looked back over the instructions and rules for when I need to bother with the elevator myself, and grabbed a cold beer out the fridge. I was going to need it. I loved how quick the cafeteria stockers were with my request.

SEVENTEEN

'That's a fine choice. Some people's desired stress reliever. It's a personal favorite and quite frankly helps me keep going. More than coffee does I must admit.'

I hadn't even thought about drinking in front of my boss. But again, this wasn't the kind of job that gave me the feeling drinking was against the rules. Before I could say anything the computer beeped, letting me know someone was buzzing my intercom.

'Uhm, hi. It's Xenna, this is where my appointment calendar told me to come.'

'Hi Xenna, come on in to the first door on the right.'

I hadn't quite practiced how to buzz someone in, so it took me a second to remember which button it was. I figured that was probably the easiest thing there was to do. Really, all of it was easy; it was just remembering what buttons controlled what.

The girl that turned the corner into my office was stunning. I was beginning to think Mr. Linguh only hired unusually pretty women. Her eyes were a sparkling blue color; they reminded me of a bright sunny beach day. How could someone with such light in there eyes be in front of me ready to end it all? She was lean and slender, slightly curvy. Her lean frame gave the illusion she was taller than she was. Her hair was cut into a messy bob, dirty blonde with bleached highlights. Ya know Ella now that I think about it, she was the kind of girl in high school that I would've thought was gorgeous, but was one of those mean girls. You know the ones who thought they were better. I mean that's just what her appearance reminded me of, I didn't know her personally or nothin'. She smelled sweet, like flowers and vanilla. That seemed to be the common smell amongst all the pretty women. All I could think was that now I would constantly associate that scent to a dirty blonde mean girl who burned herself alive in front of me.

Mr. Linguh nodded at her as she came in. I asked her if she was sure she wanted to do this before she could really get in the door good. She nodded and I went on to explain the paperwork. I made sure tp ask her after explaining the paperwork if she was sure that was what she wanted to do. Again as she signed the paperwork, and once more after she had finished. Each time she assured me, and inadvertently Mr. Linguh, that she was confident with her decision to do this.

'Okay Xenna, when you're ready let me know. Beside us, as you can see, is the elevator. Again, when you're ready, you'll get inside the elevator and push the button to go down to the first floor. Once you push that button, I can't stress this enough to you, there is no going back. The elevator will start and automatically become engulfed in flames. I don't have the ability to stop the elevator mid ride. It'll go down to the first floor and come back up. In the event that things don't uhhh, complete, as planned, I will restart the elevator for a second ride. Do you understand? Have any questions?'

I said it as if I had explained it a million times before. Afterwards Mr. Linguh told me I was a natural. It was a compliment, I guess. Certainly wasn't one I ever thought I'd be getting.

'Yes, I understand. I'm ready,' there was no hesitation at all. She seemed determined, but more so at peace. It was a bit weird. She showed no signs of nervousness or anxiety at all. I was anxious just explaining the process to her. It was a normal physical reaction; similar to the heart rate increasing when you go for a shot at the doctor or when your plane takes off. If she experienced any of this, she certainly didn't show it on the outside. I figured if I were to have checked her pulse, it would have been steady the whole time. That couldn't have been accurate from a scientific standpoint, but I wasn't a scientist. I observed behavior, and hers showed no sign of stress. Definitely unpredictable behavior, I would have never thought that would be the case for someone who was about to cease to exist. Someone who KNEW they were about to cease to exist at that.

Mr. Linguh got up and walked over towards me, stopping by the one-way mirror. Before he could get fully adjusted, Xenna had already pushed the button. My heart rate increased. I wasn't expecting her to

SEVENTEEN

just hop right in and smack the button like she was going down to a hotel lobby or something. It startled me; I wanted to scream as if I were the one burning. Silence. There was no scream, no cry, not even a yelp of shock when the flames swiftly overtook the elevator. My mouth dropped open. I wasn't ready, but I guess I wasn't really the one who needed to be. My eyes were wide in shock. It had happened so quickly I didn't even have time to process that things had started. It wasn't like when I did a practice run the day before and two minutes seemed like two hours as I stood there staring into the burn. This seemed to be over before it even started.

The elevator beeped as it reached the second floor, jolting it's way back to it's starting position again. The flames left as quickly as they came and all that remained of the beautiful blue-eyed girl was the ash of her lean figure and faint strands of her dirty blonde bob.

'Yeah, definitely a natural,' that was all Mr. Linguh said for a moment. 'You did well, Lebannon. The shock on your face goes away after a few times. As you can see, it happens pretty quickly so eventually, you wont even remember people were going into the elevator during your shift.' With that he headed out the door, calling back for me to chat him if I needed anything. I headed to the refrigerator in the snack room. Grabbed a bottle out of the fridge and a cup from the counter, I needed something a bit stronger than a beer. But I had gotten through it, if that's what you want to to call watching a girl burn to death in front of your eyes."

EIGHTEEN

"Something about the peace that came over Xenna and the swift actions that lead to her death made me think it wasn't so bad. Mr. Linguh was right; it was over just as soon as it happened. When the elevator cooled, it was back to being the blank, soot filled view I had become accustomed to.

After Xenna, I had a balance of about five to ten consistent chatters a day, and I ranged between one to two burns a week. Sometimes I didn't see anyone, sometimes I might do three. But I don't recall ever having more than three burns in one week's time. Time trucked along around me and before I knew it I had gotten used to it all. The elevator appointment notifications didn't bother me anymore. I had come to terms with the fact that not everyone wanted to be saved. I definitely wasn't the one to go around trying to play the savior either. That would have only made things more stressful for me.

Everyday became redundant. Granted, I never really knew what I was going to get, but I at least knew what I was going to get. If that makes since."

"Wait," I interrupted him. "So, you mean, you just stopped caring that people were burning in front of you? You stopped having any feeling of concern or remorse for these people?" I couldn't wrap my head around it. There was no way I could imagine being okay with one person's taking their own life in front of me, let alone multiple people.

Maybe he had some sort of narcissistic personality disorder, because what else could explain it?

"Well Ella, I thought that's how I would feel. After a few months though, I realized for my own personal mental health, I needed to change my perspective. You see, I didn't know these people before they buzzed into my office to get in the elevator. Dare I say, I didn't care about them then, because I didn't know them. It was either me and my mind, or them. The way I saw it, they were going to take their life anyway. Whether I was there or not. They all had their minds made up, and whether it was me or some other fool, it wouldn't have changed the outcome.

Once I realized that, things were easy. Easier anyway. Plus, I didn't have to sit there and stare at it happen from beginning to end. When it was done right, it was as if there was someone in my office who just left. I was no more the wiser. Unless I sat thinking about it of course. But why should I have to do that? A trash man probably doesn't' enjoy the act of picking up dumpsters day in and day out; but it's good money so they figure it's not that bad. This really wasn't different. Not from a business perspective anyway."

I kind of understood, from that tiny little twisted place in my own soul. If Lebannon didn't teach me anything else throughout the course of that day, he definitely showed me that everyone has a small inkling of twisted in them somewhere. But the rest of me, the 98.5% of me that was morally rational, couldn't wrap my mind around it. I liked to believe that no amount of money would be worth the blood of others on my hands. But it wasn't my battle to fight, and I figured it caught up to him eventually.

"So…" I wasn't sure how to word exactly what I wanted to say so I trailed off until I found the words to say. "So, you did your six months, and it was over: I don't see how that ended you up here? I mean, if what you say is true about working for BLKQ then I am inclined to believe that they probably wouldn't want you sharing that information. But I'm still not sure of how you ended up here."

"That's the thing. It wasn't just six months."

EIGHTEEN

"I don't understand, I thought your contract was six months."

"It was. Those few weeks turned into a few months, before I knew it my contract was up. At that point, things were going great. As great as they could be anyway. Claire and I were getting closer; not talking about work was helping. My bank account and credit score were great. I was able to walk in stores and buy things without being concerned about the price. My finances were working for me. When the six-month mark hit, I looked back at the numbers and doing a few more months didn't seem like a bad idea.

That's what I thought. And every time the end of the contract drew near, that's how I felt. So I kept going. Looking back though, I got greedy. I got greedy and my pride wouldn't let me admit it to anyone. That pride was my demise; it's what contributed to me being now. My pride locked me up with a bunch of nutcases and now the only real interaction I get is sitting here talking to some intern, no offense. That's my take anyway."

"How do you mean?" There was a tiny sting at him calling me "some intern." I was still holding on to the flirtatious gestures we exchanged though we had well since moved past that. If we were on a legitimate date, and the circumstances were different, I would have found it all misleading. It would have definitely been a red flag if I were interested in dating him. But we weren't dating; I was just listening to his story. I had no right to feel betrayed now that what I perceived as flirtation was gone.

"I got used to it. With every day that went by, I got used to chatting with people to talk about how they were feeling. Slowly, I lost the true desire to help people. Behind the screen, I could present myself as a caring therapist without having to change my micro expressions. I could say the things that people just wanted to hear, whether I meant them or not. I got used to it. It was a role I played, and I played it well.

Mr. Linguh talked to me more and more. I honestly felt like sometimes I was his own personal therapist too. He checked on me constantly though, made sure I was doing okay. He seemed to genuinely care about me. I wouldn't be surprised if it was just because of how large the investment was in me. But boy did I find out that couldn't have been further from the truth. Well, maybe a little of the truth. Anyway. Would you believe me if I told you I became the longest lasting person in that department?"

"I'm not sure, I guess it depends on how long you lasted, but I could see it."

"The guy I replaced was supposedly the longest running SEA before me, he lasted exactly six months. SEA is what we abbreviated Suicide Elevator Assistant with. It sounded more welcoming. I remember when I got the balls to ask Mr. Linguh what happened to him one day.

'Well Lebannon, ironically, the elevator was how he chose to deal with stress. Hopefully the whisky you keep stored in here is your way.'"

"He got in the elevator?!" I wasn't too sure why that shocked me the way it did. I'd probably get in the elevator too if that were my job. Swallow pills, pull the trigger, something. I was only inclined to believe it would drive me to suicide too.

"Sure did. Least that's what Mr. Linguh say he did. I ended up staying in that position for about three years."

"You watched people commit suicide for three years?!"

"Well Ella, technically yes, but that wasn't really the majority of my job in total. It was definitely the messiest part, to say the least. It could have easily been the most traumatizing, even in small capacities. But I learned to deal with that part, and after a while it didn't really bother me."

"Soooo, what happened then?"

"Well, in my head I thought everything was going well. My bank account was flourishing, things with Claire seemed to be going pretty good, and then things sorta shifted. I really blame Claire for it, at some point I wanted to throw Mr. Linguh in the elevator myself. Hurt can do that sort of thing to you. Let's just say it was the perfect storm.

EIGHTEEN

I was never one to be jealous. I don't even believe myself to have been one who was insecure. You'd think given the daddy issues I had growing up I would be, but that wasn't the case. I was nonchalant. Maybe a little too nonchalant, with everything.

Claire and I had been doing whatever we were doing for a few years. I was comfortable, and she seemed to be too. Did I love her? I like to think I did. But I wasn't in a position to think about long-term future commitments, and she never seemed to press the issue herself. We were just riding the wave if you will.

One morning, after Claire had spent the night, she left her phone beside the bed. She said she had to be in the office early for some meeting. I didn't have any appointments for the day and planned to go in a little later. She rushed out earlier than she ever had before, but I didn't think much of it. I noticed her phone on the nightstand as I went to get in the shower. 'Ill drop it off to her when I head into the office, she will probably need a coffee so I'll pick her up one of those too.'

That's what I thought to myself. I was never one to go through someone else's phone, and like I said I wasn't one to be jealous. Don't look for anything, you won't find anything. That's what I liked to believe, and it worked for me.

In the shower, I heard her phone ring a few times. I didn't think much of it. Getting out the shower, I heard it ring again. I wrapped a towel around my waste and walked over to the nightstand, cringing because I hated walking on the plush carpet before I had fully dried my body. The fact of the matter was though; her phone was getting on my nerves. I had forgotten to turn music on when I got in the shower, which happened from time to time. When it did, I just assumed it was a day where I needed a little peace and quiet before I went in to work. That was one of those days and her phone was interrupting that.

GuhBear. That was what rang on the phone. GuhBear with a black heart. That didn't make much since to me. I hadn't really met many of her friends, but I hadn't heard anything remotely close to this before. Ding. Ding. Ding. Text messages kept coming in:

This morning was amazing, I really hate when you have to stay with him.

Let's do it again in the office ☺

You've done what I asked years ago, can we talk about ending it now?

He really didn't need a chaperone anyway.

I need my wife back full time."

"Wait, huh? Did I miss something?" I stuttered before he could even get his thoughts out. Things escalated quickly and I wasn't quite sure what had happened. I needed him to go back and clarify what he was telling me.

"Apparently I missed something," there was a twinge of sarcasm tied up with pain in his voice. "A wave of emotions suddenly towered over me as the wires in my brain worked in overdrive connecting the dots. Office? Chaperone? This morning? Guh? WIFE? It was as if the current flowing though it trying to make sense of what I was seeing was frying my brain. At the same time, my heart was being crushed by the wave, dragging along an ocean floor scrapping against the rocks at the bottom."

He paused, inhaling deeply. I took the opportunity to share the conclusions I had come to. My neurons too were firing away trying to figure out what was going on. "Are you telling me Claire was married to Linguh?!"

The ways his mouth twisted hearing someone else say it out loud told me everything I needed to know. I was right.

He finally let out a loud sigh. He must have been holding that same breath since I blurted out my thoughts on the situation, "That was the conclusion I came to. It made sense, given the context clues. She didn't live with me or anything, and I had never actually been to her place.

Either way, no matter what was what, those texts let me know that not only was she not faithful to me, SHE WAS MARRIED! My brain was firing a million neurons a minute, trying to figure out the best course of action. My heart though, my heart had made it to places more vulnerable than I thought it had. Stuck between the scrubbing of the ocean floor and the pressure of the wave, I felt my heart break into trillions of tiny little pieces.

The funny thing about heartbreak, it comes based on many different emotions. My heart didn't shatter at the thought of losing her. It wasn't because I felt all the memories we shared were a lie, though to me they were. It wasn't like we had ever talked or planned some elaborate future together. Naw, my heart broke under the pressure of betrayal. No we weren't talkin' about marriage, kids, and a house on the hills or nothing; but I had a pretty good feelin' we were at least goin' steady. Not to mention, what was it about a chaperone? Was I some sort of project between her and Mr. Linguh to keep me in my right mind to fill the position? I just didn't understand."

I could tell the emotions were still raw for him, even after all this time. His voice cracked a little. If that was the event that sent him into a cascade finally landing him here, with me, in a sterile white room: I understood.

"I agree, heartbreak can be one heck of a thing. Even your own mind can be a terrible contributor to how the heart breaks. I've never been through something as drastically painful as what you're describing. I'd like to believe I would handle it like a champ, but emotions and feelings are just too unpredictable. I hadn't even thought about all the underlying emotions that can cause heartbreak. So many different factors." I paused for a moment. I was curious, but found myself battling with how blunt to be. Should I just ask what I wanted to know? Or wait until he finally finished the story? I voted on blunt, what he heck right? "So, what happened? What did you do? I can only assume it was true if you say Mr. Linguh is the reason you ended up here."

For a while, there was only the sound of the cards slapping against one another. The flutter of them being shuffled, smacked, then shuffled again. There was also a small, faint sound of what I could only assume was snoring coming from Ron. I turned my head to check on him, I hadn't bothered to the entire time. Lebannon had stolen all of my attention. There was a brief moment where I remembered that the least least, I could do as an intern was check on the other patient in the room. By check, all I did was look at him from the comfort of where I was sitting. I had given up my internship, at least for the day anyway.

"It took me a little while to decide what exactly I wanted to do. I prided myself on being a pretty easy-going guy, but this really did mess me up. I paced the room for a while. Walking back and forth around my bed to the bathroom door and back again. Obviously I couldn't call her then because I had her phone. That was probably her saving grace. I didn't have a means to deal with her at least until I got to work. It gave me time to think. I'd like to say calm down, but I don't think I really calmed down from it for a while. I decided that I wanted to continue to be the nonchalant, easy-going guy. There was never a reason for her to know how difficult anything was going in my life, and I wasn't gonna start with that. Not by any means. It was clear her feelings for me were just a grand performance. I wasn't going to give her the validation that she had done a good job.

I wanted to be as smooth as possible. I must admit. I wanted to seem completely unbothered. The way I saw it, there was no way she had kept the charade going for years without developin' some sort of connection. And if she did, well I'll be that girl deserves an award. Anyways, I got myself together. Made sure I looked damn good too. Stopping by the large mirror in the entryway, I looked myself over then headed out.

I really wish I would have had the whole time to prepare like I should have, but things didn't quite go as planned."

"You lost it?"

"Well, no. I wasn't plannin' to see her 'till I got to work. She must have realized she forgot her phone and came back. As I walked toward my parking spot, I got a glimpse of her getting out of her car. She was smiling that dull fake smile she had held for the past three years. Had

EIGHTEEN

it been the day before, I would have assumed she was happy to see me again or something. This time, not so much. I was on to the rouse.

'Hey! I totally forgot my phone here,' she was giggling. I didn't know if it was real nervousness, but I figured not. She had hidden the elaborate lie for so long how could she have possibly thought anything of it. Once you've gotten away with the same thing over and over, the anxiety or fear of getting caught decreases.

The rage inside of me was a beast. It was as if every being of my heart grew ten times bigger, building into a massive fire of rage that wanted to take the spotlight. I took a deep breath, trying to push down that fire. I tried hard to smother it with my pride. It worked.

Giving her the coldest, uninterested look ever I said, 'Yeah here it is. Oh yeah, your husband called and texted quite a few times too. Think he may want to see you when you finally make it to the office.' With that, I opened my car door, got in, and backed away. I left her there, frozen in time with a look of pure horror on her face. She was so stuck she couldn't find words to say quick enough. There was no fumbling around with what to say, just a blank stare as I drove away. Her mouth slightly opened in shock.

I drove away feeling like THE MAN."

I laughed aloud. It was like going back in time. The way he chose to describe some things was quite articulate. Other things he chose to use dated slang. Hearing him boisterously say "the man," that was hilarious to me. I understood, of course, I just also knew it was a dated phrase. The same way he said Claire and he were going steady. I let that one slide, but my tickle box just couldn't let this one go. It was a bit infectious obviously, because when I looked up, wiping the tears from my eyes that had formed, he was giggling.

"What's so funny?" He managed to get out in between chuckles.

"Oh nothing, you da man," I hollered again at my own joke. "Okay, okay. I'm sorry. So, what happened after "the man" drove off?"

It took a second for both of us to stop giggling. Finally, we were composed enough for him to go on. "I stopped by the café anyway, even though I definitely wasn't getting Claire that coffee. I got an iced coffee. I could have gotten one at work; the cafeteria literally had everything I could want, coffee included. I needed the café taste though. I got to work, went through the back entrance, and got started on the tasks I had for the day.

The distraction was really nice actually. There were more chats that day than there had been in a while. I was able to focus on other people's problems. That wasn't the best way to deal with it in hindsight. I buried my problems underneath everyone else's. The more chats I received, the more I felt good about the decision to bury my heartbreak."

"Did she not try to reach out to you or come to your office? What about Mr. Linguh? Did he ever say anything?"

"Oh, she did. I'm not real sure if she was trying to save face or what, but she was blowing up my phone. She kept askin' to talk, saying she could explain. She even chatted me through the company app. She never used that thing, at least not with me. I left her on read for a while. Pretty much all day. I did finally text her a few days later and let her know I wasn't interested in talkin' and she was free to get back to her marriage as her husband wanted.

I was cold. I don't know if it came off harsh to her or not, I was just being blunt. I didn't really care. As far as Mr. Linguh, it was weeks before he said anything to me. He pretty much avoided me like the plague. I found myself wondering from time to time what type of strain that mess up may have put on their relationship."

"What did he say?"

"Finally, he came into my office one evening. I was there late because I had a late elevator appointment. I believe it was one of the night shifters that was coming in early. Around that time a new trafficking ring was coming on the scene, moving quickly. That alone made the office more hectic than normal. They were more aggressive and had far less up keeping standards than most of the other rings that Department L saw. Daily there were hundreds of children flashing across the screens.

EIGHTEEN

Some were even babies. That started to strike a few more nerves. Not to mention there was a number of newer employees, and that was their first new ring rush.

Anyway, he had stayed late that evening. 'Hey, it's uhh Linguh. Can I come in and talk with you for a bit?' He was at the speaker on the outside of my department door. I guess it was decent of him to ask, even though I knew he could have just walked in at any time. He owned the place.

'Yeah, come on in.' I buzzed him in, again realizing that he could have done that himself.

'Like what you've done with the place, it's been a while. You've been doing great in this department. You've lasted much longer than I could have imagined. You must find a really good way to deal with stress.' He was beating around the bush and fishing, all at the same time. All his accolades were misguided and layered behind an embarrassing attempt to make a mends. He was Mr. Linguh. Mr. Linguh knew how to compliment, he knew how to commend without it coming off as ass kissing.

'Yeah, I reckon it's come a way since you been in here last. I deal the best way I know how. How're things out on the floors?'

'Oh, most have been quiet, at least as quiet as it can be around here. Department L is really a shit show right now though. The newbies and the influx of trafficking sales, let's just say it's crazy.' He sounded more like himself when he talked about what was happening around the facility, not like the imposter he came in as.

'Yeah, I bet.'

It got quiet for a minute. I really wasn't interested in the fake pleasantries, but the reality was he was my boss. I looked at him as such. Honestly, at that point I had buried everything deep down and started to live a new normal. Without Claire, without thinking about the terrible situation BLKQ had landed me in life. Instead, I was thinking about the ups. The pros, not the cons. I wish it had stayed that way. Mr. Linguh stopping by that night to talk, it unearthed things that should have stayed far underneath the pile of nonsense I had put on top of it."

NINETEEN

"Mr. Linguh sat there for a while, not saying anything. Pulling one of the chairs from the small sitting area out to the middle of the office, he sat down fidgeting with his fingers. After a few minutes of awkward silence, he finally spoke. 'Listen, uhhh Lebannon. I want to explain a few things to you. I know I've been avoiding you for a while now, and that's definitely not something I typically do. This situation is uhmm, unique. Honestly, I've never found myself in this situation before. So uhh, I wanted to finally come and talk to you, hoping to clear things up.'

He stumbled across his words a lot. It was quite out of character for him. I must admit, watching him stumbled around in conversation was oddly satisfying, and equally pitiful. Had I intimidated him?

'Ok, let me just cut to the chase here Lebannon.' That was more like it. 'When I offered the internship to you, I already knew your resume and capabilities. Riley and I have been good friends for a long while now. I knew you were going to be a good fit, but as you already know I don't really run a business on ordinary practices. That being said, yes Claire is my wife. We have been married for a while now. I got her to get close to you as an inside person that could help you handle the stress of the job. I really needed you if I'm to be blunt.'

'She couldn't have simply befriended me like a normal person?'

'Well, yeah I guess she could've . But we figured if you knew she was my wife it might not hold the same weight.'

I was confused, to say the least. Either way, I could feel all the buried emotions starting to pop out of their graves one decayed arm at a time.

'Listen Mr. Linguh, I'm not to sure what type of relationship you have or how y'all get down. It really ain't too tough my business. But it's cool man. Whatever y'all had going on, it is what it is. I would have much rather preferred something be said years ago, or just being up front and honest. I'm over it. I really appreciate you coming down here to say all that, but it really ain't necessary. Least as far as I'm concerned.'

I hoped everything I said came out as smooth as I wanted it too. I silently wished upon the entire universe hoping that the decaying hand of betrayal and lies didn't escape through my words. I prayed to whatever god would hear that the tiny bouts of tension in my face went unnoticed. I wanted him to leave. My jaws clenched against one another, thrusting my teeth deeper into my gums. Things weren't going well inside of me, but I couldn't let that out in front of him.

'Look, I hope there aren't any hard feelings?' The words came out shakier than I'm sure he meant. He seemed somewhat nervous. Maybe even embarrassed.

'Naw man, not at all. Everything's good. I won't tryin' to marry the girl or nothing.' I was hoping adding that last part in subtly would strike a nerve in him. There was just a smidge of petty seeping through as all of my emotions further stretched their way from the grave I'd buried them in.

There was visible shock on his face. He tried to hide it, but I could spot micro expressions miles away. His eyebrows raised ever so slightly. His lips parted just enough to let out a small gasp. He looked around the room, confused and awkward, fidgeting with his fingers more. 'Well listen, I'm glad everything's good on your end. I'm going to check on the departments one last time and then head on out of here. Uhm, don't stay too late.'

'No worries.'

NINETEEN

Just like that, he was gone. I heard his footsteps all the way to the door leaving the hallway from my office. Hearing it slam behind him I let out a long breath. Rage and bitterness were suddenly rising inside of me, trying to escape. Unbeknownst to me, I had been holding my breath since he got up, hoping the lack of oxygen would slow their ascend long enough to keep from completely exploding in front of him. You know, I got my degree and everything, but I dealt with stress clients more than anything else. I didn't often have to uncover buried memories or take trips down memory lane with clients trying to unbury so they could heal. If the process for them felt anything like what I was experiencing, well I could completely understand why folks didn't want to go to therapists often. It was absolutely terrible!

When I felt he had gotten far enough away, I screamed. Maybe more of a yell. Mmm, probably a shriek really. It was like my heart was a bottle of soda that had been shaken and shaken and shaken. Now the top was off, and I was exploding. I stood there, choking back angry tears for about an hour. The lump in my throat seemed to grow with every deep breath I took. I was trying hard to be the calm, easygoing guy I had portrayed myself to be, but it just wasn't working. My eyes were red. Suddenly my mind was running miles a minute.

There was a fight raging inside of me, a war really. Every small or big thing that I had pushed aside for years suddenly fought its way to the front of my mind. Emotions were fighting for their shot to shine in the spotlight. I grabbed a glass of whiskey from the fridge in my snack area. I usually wasn't a stress eater, but today I felt like I wanted to eat. I poured more than a normal shot amount and chugged it like it was nothing. I didn't even feel the burn in my chest as it made it's way down into my stomach. Or maybe I did and I needed the distraction from everything else going on inside me, I'm not sure really. I did that a few more times and decided to go home instead of ordering from the cafeteria like I was going to.

I stood up, stumbling. My eyes rolled back to the elevator as my thoughts took over. I'm not sure if I was thinking about getting in myself or not. I didn't have much time to decipher what exactly I was contemplating as I stared into the keeper of incinerated souls. My thoughts were interrupted by a ding at my computer. It was the sound of an elevator appointment coming through. Jake. I actually knew Jake; we had been out for drinks a time or two. I met him at the bar actually, on one of the stressful days. I didn't know he worked there until later. Then I became a friend to him. He knew I worked with him, but he didn't know what department I was in.

He made the appointment for tomorrow morning. It was earlier than most appointments. All I could think was great, I have to wake up early. I should have been more concerned that someone who probably considered me a friend at the minimum wanted to get in the elevator. I just wasn't in a place to care about anything but what I was dealing with at the time. Had it been another day, maybe even if I wasn't drunk, I would have called him. Maybe I could have changed his mind. That's hindsight though. I'd love to sit here and tell you I was some caring guy, but I wasn't. Not really, not in that moment at least. Verdict is still out on if I am now or not.

I closed the computer and headed out the door, stumbling all the way to my car."

"You drove home, drunk?"

"Sure did. In that moment I didn't care about anything. What did I have to lose? I should have put in my resignation before letting Mr. Linguh leave. That would have been the best thing for me to do. But by the time I thought of that it was too late."

"What do you mean it was too late?"

"Well, I went home. Can't believe I got there safe, sound, and in one piece. But I did. I set my alarm and before I knew it, I was passed out on the couch. I'm a firm believer in sleeping things off. You should try it if you haven't. I figured everything would be fine in the morning and

NINETEEN

I would go back to living life calm and easy going. That didn't happen. I was more emotional in the morning than I was the night before.

I had never had so many emotions running through me at one time. I should have stayed home. I never called out before, quite frankly I don't even know if you could call out of that job. But I should have tried. I was angry, sad, frustrated, hurt, betrayed. So many things, all at once. It was as if all the emotions fighting for the spotlight the night before had equally succeeded.

I was running a little behind, my head throbbed as I shuffled around the condo trying to focus on matching a shirt and tie instead of the thumbing against my brain. I remembered that I had an appointment, but for the life of me I couldn't remember who it was with. It had been drowned in the whiskey. I showered quickly, barely drying off before jumping into my pants and trying to button my shirt as I grabbed a cup of coffee on the way out. I was going to need it."

TWENTY

"I wasn't stable. You know psychologists can make the worst patients sometimes. We tend to think we know everything. And since we do indeed know, or are at least aware, of certain symptoms and issues, we think we can manage them on our own. That was me. My pride got in the way. I shouldn't have been at work, not in the state I was in. I was in the early stages of having a complete mental breakdown. Every major stressor I had now lined the small pathway I had pushed them to the edge of. Now it seemed like they had created a mountain of problems that had gotten too high. Their weight was starting to fall into the path I was trying to walk down and with each piece that toppled on me crushed me a little more. I shouldn't have been at work. The weight of someone else's problems was bound to suffocate me, but I had gotten too used to using it as a cover. I thought I could do it again; cover up the falling tower of my own problems by focusing on someone else's.

I also shouldn't have been the one to oversee Jake in the elevator. It was a conflict of interest, similar to accepting a good friend as a patient. You just shouldn't do it. Keep that in mind now. I'm sure you will be very successful in your career, but I don't want you to make the same mistakes I did."

I tried to make light of the conversation in that moment, "Well, hopefully I don't find myself working in the shadows of the dark web."

He smiled, "I'm just sayin'. Anyway, I told you I forgot who the appointment was with until the buzzer rang for the speaker.

'It's Jake, I was given instructions to come here for my uhh... appointment.'

I buzzed him in. Sobriety took over just enough for me to be curious about what was happening with Jake, now that I remembered it was Jake. I wasn't in a place to try to save anyone. I never was, and had no plans to start that day. I was in no position to try to save anyone even if I wanted to. I was barely keeping my feet from sleeping out from under me.

He was shocked to see me when he rounded the corner. His hazel eyes almost popped out of his head. He definitely wasn't expecting me of all people. 'Lebannon? You're the elevator assistant?'

'Yeah man. Now listen, if this is really what you want to do, it's not my job to stop you. Just know I'm going to ask you a bunch of times if you're certain this is what you wanna do.' He shook his head, indicating he understood. I didn't feel the need for professional tones, moreso I was probably too hung over to use the proper terms. 'You don't have to explain to me why, or anything like that. I just need to know that you want to do this. I need you consent every time I ask.'

I went over the documents he needed to sign. Every time I asked if he was sure, he said he was. I noticed though that there seemed to be a glisten in his eyes each time he lied. It wasn't a glimmer of hope and peace like some of the clients had when they knew it was that time. Instead, I realized it was tears. He seemed like this was probably a very hard decision for him. Morally, I should have pushed him on that and really figure out if he was just scared of death or desperately needin' someone to stop him. My morality had long since gone away though, and my mind was just to get this appointment done so I could go back to wading through the waters of my own emotional discord. The cloud of whiskey fogged the region of reason within me. It fogged the desire deep down to sit and have a conversation with a friend, over more whiskey.

TWENTY

It was time. I let him know what would happen when he got in the elevator. I could see the uneasiness on his face, but it's what he told me he wanted. I had to respect that. That's what I told myself anyway. He walked over to the elevator and stepped in. Had I paid attention, I would have noticed Jake's hands shaking as he tried to hold them in front of him getting into the elevator. I would have seen his knees ever so slightly smack against one another as he stood in the elevator, overwhelmed by what he saw. I probably might have even noticed the stream of tears he had tried to hide by turning his face away from the mirror.

There was something rising inside of me. It was terrible timing. I was in the middle of an appointment, but my emotions didn't care about that. There I was again, holding my breath trying to suffocate the rising army of anger, bitterness, and betrayal long enough to get through the end of the appointment. How selfish does that sound out loud? A guy I knew on a somewhat personal level was feet away, probably close to pissin' himself, and I couldn't be bothered for a second to ask one last time. I couldn't even be bothered to let my emotions out of the cage I was trying to keep them in in hopes it would distract him. I was too prideful to let someone else see me that way. That was the only appointment I ever remember that I was solely focused on myself. A terrible time to be that selfish too.

It usually only took one try, and it was generally a short process as far as time was concerned. What I expected to be a couple minutes turned into a lifetime of being locked away with the insane."

Confusion pushed it's way out taking over my voice, 'Huh? What does Jake have to do with Mr. Linguh putting you in here?"

"I turned on the speaker so I could hear Jake. I let him know he could hit the button whenever he was ready. It took him about five minutes to push the button. Every time I think about it, I kick myself. I should have let him out. I should have at least insisted that he reschedule to give himself time to ensure that was what he really wanted to do.

Obviously, he had reserves. But eventually, he hit the button. Maybe he realized his last hope wouldn't be the savior he desperately needed.

I had overseen at least a hundred elevator experiences by the time Jake hit that button. That was by far the absolute worst. Don't get me wrong, they weren't all as smooth as the first one. Some of them were, but not all. Sometimes I had people who prayed, some made a bit more noise because of the initial shock of the flames. No two rides were the same. This was different though. It was unlike anything I had ever experienced before.

The flames started and for the first few seconds, everything was fine. Before I knew it I jumped, startled by a glass shattering scream. My heart started pounding and for a split second I forgot who I was and what I was doing. I snapped back to reality and realized Jake was screaming. It was a murderous scream. That sound was horrendous! I didn't even know anything like it existed

'Help me! Help me! I don't want to do this anymore. Please. PLEASE! Stop it, STOP IT! Nooooooo!'

The desperation in his voice was the stressor the crushed me on that little path. It was the straw that broke the camel's back and all of a sudden, I wanted it to stop. I understood him, in that moment. I, too, wanted it to stop. I wanted the pile of stressors suddenly holding my breath hostage beneath their power to let me go. More importantly I was desperate to right the wrong of not taking his cues and micro expressions into consideration. I was wrong for not being the friend he had saw me as. We weren't the best of buds or anything, but he had trusted me with secrets. He should have been able to count on me, even if it was a last resort. Right in the knick of time.

My fingers screamed in agony as I found myself scratching at the elevator's doors. 'I don't know how! I'm trying! I'm trying Jake!' I was desperate to help him. So desperate. I needed his screams to stop. For a minute and a half, I tried to get in the elevator, to no avail. Blood seeped out of the cuts I had made in my fingers against the door as my palms

TWENTY

burned. It didn't matter. The elevator was built not to be interrupted. There was a lone panic button that went directly to Mr. Linguh on the control panel. In all the disarray and chaos, I must have hit it.

I've replayed it all over and over and it never ceases to amaze me how many small details I remember. Saying it out loud, for the first time in a while, now I recall getting up from the dirty floor in front of the elevator racing through my office door to the control panel. I tried helplessly to stop the elevator. Surely there was SOMETHING that could make it stop. I always seemed to skip over that part in my mind though. The way it plays out on the screen behind my eyes, I was in front of that elevator door the entire time. Banging, beating, and pleading it to let me in, not even thinking through what I would do with the flames if I were able to get in.

The elevator dinged, letting me know it had made it to the second floor. I switched it off, making sure it didn't go for another ride. I smashed the door override key that allowed me to open the doors even when it was still hot. Rushing around the corner from my office to the elevator doors, I couldn't believe it. The elevator hadn't worked, it must have been a miracle only Jake could have prayed for. The elevator never failed on the first ride, not in the hundreds of times before. He was burned, for sure, but he was still alive. His screams had become muffled, probably due to soot and smoke taking up space in his lungs. I'll never forget that low, dry cry. It was so raspy and desperate. I don't know what was worse, the gut wrenching scream of utter desperation, or the low raspy cry slowing dying out in front of me. They both terrorize my nightmares just the same.

It was hot. Snatch the breath out of you hot. I had never actually opened the doors before the temperature dropped back to normal and had no idea of what to expect. It didn't matter. I was determined to get him out. I could still hear the deafening screams in my head even though they had since calmed to a whispering wail. I thought if I just got him out, it would stop.

Mr. Linguh ran into the entryway right as I went in the elevator to get Jake.

'What the hell are you doing, Lebannon? What happened? What's going on?' I don't know if he really was screaming, but I heard screams. I saw everything chaotic and fast. But it was slow at the same time. Slow motion.

I didn't feel the burn of my arm and hand," he touched the arm that I noticed was scarred earlier. "My focus was on getting Jake out. I grabbed him and yanked his body outside of the elevator.

'I have to get him out! He didn't really want this, he wanted to stop it!' I was screaming at Mr. Linguh who was telling me to let him go. I was hysterical by that point. I completely lost it. My arms thrashed around, trying to break free of the grasp Mr. Linguh had on me. He was trying to get me off of Jake. 'He doesn't want to die! We have to save him! I was screaming louder than I probably intended to, but I just couldn't seem to say it loud enough. To me, it seemed like my words were stuck in my throat and everytime I opened my mouth nothing came out. My voice cracked with a desperation similar to what I heard from Jake inside the elevator. 'I'm going to tell everyone what you've done! You killed him! The world is going to know what you do here you ASSHOLE!'

I must have blacked out. I had Jake; his shoulders were locked under my arms. I swore I had gotten him out of the elevator. 'Jake wae up! WAKE UP! You're out. You're out! Linguh you're going to burn in hell for this...' Maybe those were the last things I said before darkness poured over me like a fresh pot of coffee. Maybe I said more, either way I knew better. I knew what my job was, and my emotional state jeopardized my ability to objectively deal with that appointment. I should have called out. I shouldn't have stayed so long. So many should've could've would'ves."

He trailed off, with a blank stare in his eyes. At least, it seemed blank. Looking a little deeper, it wasn't so blank. It was, mysterious.

TWENTY

Broken. Longing. Maybe he really did wish he could go back and change the situation.

"So, what happened next?" I was apprehensive. I didn't know if I wanted to break the barrier of silence that had seated itself among us. My chest was still tight from the horrible recount of events Lebannon had just given.

"Well. What happened next is I woke up in the loveliest hotel room I've ever been in." He smiled. "In case you can't pick up on sarcasm, that was it. The lovely hotel room I landed myself in was right down the hall there," he pointed towards the door.

"I don't understand, you woke up here?"

"Yes Ella. I woke up here. Mr. Linguh wasn't the type of man you threatened, and he didn't really believe in forgiving graces when it came to someone who could potentially ruin his business. I can only imagine he didn't take kindly to the things I said during my mental fiasco and it landed me here.

I guess it could have been worse. Given his shady business, I would have been certain that he had the ability to get me killed, no problem. Hell, he could have very well tossed me and Jake back into that elevator and turned it on. Who would have been the wiser? But he didn't. Sometimes I wish he had."

The room fell silent again. Wow. This was all pretty heavy. I had been sitting there for hours with a man who was in an insane asylum, listening to him recount some of the most horrible things I had ever heard. The biggest factor was oh, I don't know, him being in a mental facility. But even still, he was normal. He didn't seem to have any ticks, and that entire time there was nothing about him that lead me to believe he was lying. I should have thought he was lying, but I didn't. I believed him. I felt for him actually. I couldn't imagine what it must have been like to go through all of that. It must have been his charm and friendly demeanor. Maybe it was the educated verbiage he used from time to time. Could have even been those flirtatious gestures we started with.

Whatever it was, something about him proved to be trustworthy as I sat across from him, clinging on to his every terrible word.

I was trying to digest everything. *Was this why I had to sign an NDA when I first got here? Was the staff in Mr. Linguh's pocket as well? Was everything still being dealt with through Mr. Linguh after all this time? Was he supposed to stay in here the rest of his life?* There were so many pressing questions. I decided to ask the one that was at the forefront of my mind.

"Well, uhm, do you know what happened to Jake?"

It took him a few minutes to respond. I didn't press him; I had learned earlier in the day to just let him answer my questions on his own time. He took a deep breath, "Well Ella, he's still alive. Though I must admit I'm sure at this point he would have much rather died in that elevator. I often wonder if he blames me for saving him. For dragging him out of that fiery elevator and sentencing him to a life worse than the fate he had chosen, before he changed his mind." He trailed off again for a moment. He took his hand, the one covered in scars, and lifted it to his face, squishing his eyes with his thumb and index finger for a moment before rubbing his temples. "Jake's full name is Jacory Dinson."

"Jacory?" I couldn't mask the shock in my voice. I looked around frantically, glancing over and over again towards the door. "Jacory as in the guy who had an episode this morning thinking someone was going to kill him? That Jacory?"

Another long sigh, "Yes. That Jacory. They locked him away in here too."

"Why haven't you tried to tell anyone what happened?" I didn't realize my voice had raised slightly.

"Shh," he looked around. "Do you think anyone would believe me? Did you believe Jacory when you saw him spazzing this morning? There's no reason. There's no hope in trying to tell anyone. It would just be a waste of time. There's nothing we can do about it, and it really is what it is."

I couldn't believe that could be the case. But deep down, I knew he was right. "So why did you tell me? How do you know I'm not going to leave here when my shift is over and tell the police?"

TWENTY

"I'm sure you may be inclined to Ella, but you won't. You can't really. This is a dangerous game and to play it, you could very well lose that pretty little smile of yours. I can't tell you what to do. And if you believe me, man that's great. But I didn't tell you because I need some sort of savior to get the information to someone on the outside. I told you because you listened. You gave me the opportunity to let it all out, and for the most part you were judgment free," he smiled. "I encourage you to keep all this information to yourself. Mr. Linguh and his people are dangerous. Very dangerous. Maybe I was afforded some special treatment because I was a long-time employee. You obviously don't have that kind of favor on your side with this."

"But what happened to your money? Can't you just bribe your way out of here?" I was surprised at how desperately I wanted to free this man. He'd definitely pulled at a few invisible heartstrings. That was more than I could say for any other guy in my life over the past few years.

"My money is locked away in an account. It doesn't matter though. I'm not interested in getting out."

"Huh? You're not?"

"No. Ella I didn't live a good life when I was out there. I don't have any friends. The one girl who I considered to have had a relationship with, well you know how that went. I made all that money. I convinced myself that I was just going to work long enough to make a little come up. I did more than that. And you know, when I was at the top; I didn't have much to show for it. It wasn't worth it in the long run," he leaned back in his chair, folding his arms across his chest. I could only imagine that was something he picked up from his many talks with Mr. Linguh over the years. "I'm content in here. I help look after the others like Jake and Ron, and I don't have any worries. I don't mind being in here Ella, so please don't leave with the idea of trying to rescue me."

I was stuck at his last statement. Confused that he thought I was trying to save him and wondering how he knew I actually wanted to.

"Oh, my dear Ella, I am so sorry, hun!" Candy came rushing into the Rec Room adjusting her clothes. Had she been screwing her boyfriend this whole time? It was pretty much the end of the day. "I got Jacory to his room and got sidetracked, please forgive me I completely forgot I sent you in here sweetheart."

"It's no problem at all," the old rickety chair squeaked as my weight shifted. It leaned a little as I used the arm rests to push my body from the seat across from Lebannon. I looked at him, reading his eyes. He longed for me to keep quiet. I hoped he understood that I would.

"I hope Lebannon wasn't too much of a burden for you today," Candy walked me towards the front entrance. She said she would let me go home early since she had basically left me majority of the day. "He can be quite the storyteller. Don't take it to heart, he has quite the imagination. See you tomorrow morning. Promise I won't forget you then!"

She waved me off as I retreated back through the same dingy doors that I entered hours earlier. The receptionist was no more pleasant upon my departure, and that was fine.

The entire walk to my car, I kept wondering why Candy said Lebannon had quite the imagination? Did she know he was going to tell me the story of how he ended up at Henry Ellin? Had she heard it herself? Or was it a coy plot to remind me where he was so I would be discouraged from believing him at all?

I looked back at the building toward the window where I had sat most of the day with Lebannon. To my surprise, there he was, watching me through the same window. He had an odd smile on his face. It wasn't the same smile I had watched spread across his face for hours. It was different. It looked a little sinister, maybe a little eerie. It must have just been the cloudiness of the old dirty window. I figured he was just happy to have had someone listen to him. I smiled and waved goodbye.

He walked away from the window, without waving back.

TWENTY-ONE

Wow. It had been quite the day. I could't quite seem to wrap my mind around what all had happened. It certainly wasn't the first day of internship I had expected, granted my expectations were extraordinarily low. Non-existent really. Sitting in my room, I felt a little uneasy. I wasn't exactly sure what was happening, so I did what I always do when I feel uneasy. I sat there, closed my eyes, and tried to sort out all the different thoughts and emotions inside of me.

The plush carpet was surprisingly comfortable at the foot of my bed, at least compared to their chair I had sat in all day listening to Lebannon. Crossing my legs, I took a deep breath, closed my eyes, then exhaled. Now it was time to sort through my thoughts. I started with what all had happened throughout the day. I showed up for the internship, met a very kind lady Candy, and got to experience firsthand a few different mental patients. They were all different. None of that compared to my experience throughout the day with Lebannon.

I remembered why I was originally drawn to him. He was peculiar, mysterious. There was a flash of remembrance across my eyes, his handsome features sitting at the table. He stuck out like a sore thumb amongst the other patients who were clearly incapacitated. I could almost hear the attractive, twangy voice appeal to me across the room. "I hate to break it to ya Ella." That was the first thing he said to me. He was the only patient among the few I had encountered that spoke to me, first at that. Oh yes, I wanted to try to diagnose him. Was that it? Was I uneasy because I didn't successfully diagnose him?

No, that wasn't it. He was captivating. I must admit. Maybe it had something to do with my sudden desire to learn more about his story than trying to diagnose him. Yeah, that was something. How could I be a successful therapist or counselor if I got too caught up in the story of the patient?

That was all true, but it didn't fit the bill. This uneasy feeling was more than the potential that I might fail as someone's therapist one day. Surely, I wouldn't be in the same situations again, but who knows. This was more than that. I thought back to Lebannon. The things he said. He shared some pretty dark stuff with me today, but why? Why did he trust me, a stranger, with such intimate details of his life? Why was he so eager to tell me the things that lead to him being placed in Henry Ellin? Not to mention, why was it so easy for me to forget he was a patient to begin with?

I believed him, was that it? Could it have been my ease in believing his dark experiences, taking what he said at face value? I racked my brain, meditating for a while. Sorting through each and every question in my head. It was a frustrating process, but I couldn't sleep. I kept feeling like there was something I was missing. The uneasiness just wouldn't let up.

Lebannon had told me he didn't want to be saved. He didn't want to be rescued from the punishment of his past life. I wanted to respect that. I genuinely believed that what he shared with me was something that needed to be shared, but not acted on. He just wanted to share his story with someone, but why me? Why a random intern? Surely he could have shared this with anyone else before I came along.

Soon it hit me. I remembered the eerie smile he gave me through the window. I tried hard to piece everything together in my mind. What happened exactly? I tried hard to bring back that moment to the

TWENTY-ONE

forefront of my mind, taking each step all over again as I stared on from behind my eyelids.

It was chilly when I walked outside. I wasn't sure if it was because I had been in the warm building all day, or if it was actually the temperature. The wind blew, it was a crisp breeze filling my nose with fresh air. I walked across the grounds to where my car was parked but slowed down slightly as I approached my car. Why? Why did I slow down? There it was. I had a strange feeling of someone watching me. I felt as if there was someone staring at me from the distance and inadvertently slowed my pace. I should have sped up, at least that's what I thought I should have done if that's how I felt. But I didn't, my feet slowly dragged along instead. I must have remembered the view from the Rec Room overseeing my car because I looked directly up at the window. I didn't look to my right or left to see if there was someone at my level that may have been looking at me. Instead, my head tilted up as my eyes instantly fell on the dusty clouded Rec Room window.

There he was. Standing in the window he looked completely different. The handsomely mysterious man whom I had spent hours sitting in front of was now staring at me. But it didn't feel the same. His eyes pierced through me. It was almost as if the mysterious man I knew was replaced by someone who looked just like him. He stared at me with intent satisfaction. His facial expression was intense, and his smile was twisted. It was dark.

I pulled myself back to reality. Why had looking at Lebannon felt cold as I thought about it sitting in my room? Something was off. When it occurred, I had brushed off the creepy view of him. The glass must have just been dirty, distorting what I was seeing. Maybe my eyes had been playing tricks on me. Now, I wasn't so sure that was the case. What was it Candy had said? Lebannon had an active imagination or something. A sense of dread came over me, who had I really spent the day with? Was his story true? The notion was deafening, loudly screaming at me for having been a fool. Horror crept over me as visions of something horrible circled my brain.

I jumped up, hitting my knee on the side of the bed. I didn't have time to deal with the pain. My laptop was lighter than I remembered as I snatched it towards me. I wasn't exactly sure what to search for. I racked my brain, going back through the filing cabinets filled with today's occurences as I had filed them away. You could find anything on the Internet, if it was there to be found. I took a deep breath then started typing:

Suicide Elevator

There couldn't be that much on the Internet about a suicide elevator. I was certain typing it in the search engine would help me figure out something about Lebannon. Even knowing that his job was dark web based, and that he never found reviews about working there; I still typed away in the search engine. There had to be something about him. The things he didn't share, what he didn't want me to know. What I found was definitely not what I bargained for. The search results popped up. My heart suddenly sank into my stomach. It fell from it's spot in my chest so quickly nausea started to overtake me. There were more results than I expected to find:

Prolific serial killer blames suicide elevator for deaths of hundreds.

Lebannon Smith declared insane after murdering over 100 men and women.

Serial killer sentenced to life in mental health facility for over 100 murders.

Serial killer says he was saving murder victims by helping them commit suicide.

Warm salty tears made their way down my chin, dropping onto my shirt when there was nothing more to roll on. My entire body was numb, as if emotions were holding every organ hostage, muffling the ability to feel. Overwhelming dread wrapped me up. I didn't understand. Had I

TWENTY-ONE

just spent the day with a serial killer? Was he playing some game with my mind all day? I clicked on the first article:

Prolific serial killer blames suicide elevator for deaths of hundreds.

June 18, 2008

Authorities were alerted late Friday evening of a potential crime scene on Hormer Blvd at the home of Lebannon Smith, 25. Reports indicate one potential victim escaped, alerting police of Smith's home and basement where victim claims Smith intended to burn him alive.

When police and crime scene detectives arrived, Smith seemed to be in a full mental breakdown, admitting to helping over one hundred victims commit suicide in what he claims was their desire to be free.

I was sick. I couldn't believe what I was reading. For an hour I wrecked myself desperately going through every online article and news clip I could. Suddenly I remembered Jacory and quickly typed his name in the search engine. There was a short video, it looked like an interview with Jacory:

"*Jacory, you've been through quite the ordeal recently. Tell us, what was it like?*"

"*Man, that's a loaded question.*" It was the voice of the same man I had heard desperately trying to make Candy and the other workers aware of his danger earlier. I looked at him, trying to remember what the guy struggling with the orderlies looked like. It was all a blur, I didn't get the best of looks at him earlier, but this could be him. His eyes seemed to be the same. "*I was leaving the grocery store when this man approached me. He talked smooth and presented himself as trustworthy. I don't really remember what he wanted, but when I turned for a split second to put a bag of groceries in the car I blacked out. I must have been hit on the head. Next thing I know, I woke up in what I later found out was a basement. It was the oddest basement I had ever been in. The walls were blue, all of them. The steel door at the top of the stairs* was worn. That wasn't the worst part though, the place was filthy. There was soot everywhere.

It smelled terrible. Like burning flesh. The odd thing about the basement though, there seemed to be a window right beside the top of the stairs. I didn't know at the time, but later the police let me know it was a one-way mirror that allowed him to, uhm, watch I guess.

I didn't know what was happening. I was confused and just trying to take in my surroundings. There was a corner that caught my attention. It seemed to be a corner that held the largest amount of soot, or ashes. Whatever it was, I was freaked out. I tried hard to keep calm and think of how I was going to get out of there. That's when I heard the guy. There was a speaker somewhere down there that he talked through.

'Jacory, I saw in your eyes that you weren't happy. I'm here to help you.'

I had no idea what was happening. Literally, not a clue. Happy about what? Help me? I didn't understand, but he went on.

'In a few moments the room will fill with flames. They will only burn for a couple minutes, but that should be all it takes. You'll be at peace soon.' My heart rate increased, I remembered it beating so fast I had to trick my mind into thinking it was normal, so I didn't pass out. It started getting hot, real hot. I honestly have no idea how I made it out. Before I knew it, the room was engulfed in flames more brilliant than I had ever seen before. I realized they only seemed to burn the hottest against the walls. I got to the middle of the room, hoping I wouldn't die. I prayed, harder than I had ever prayed before. All I could think of was the bible story about the guys who were in a fiery furnace but didn't die.

It was hot at first. Hotter than I had ever felt anything in my life. Had I been on the other side of that mirror, I was sure I would have been able to see my face melting off. I was in pain, but I couldn't think about it. I couldn't think about how it felt like my blood was boiling underneath my skin. I couldn't think about the flames around me, threatening to overtake my entire body. All I could think of was that story. I couldn't remember the names of the characters. I couldn't remember why they were there to begin with. All I could

TWENTY-ONE

remember was that they didn't get burned up. I often wonder if God heard my silent cries to be like them, to not get burned up.

I must have thought about that until the flames subsided. I realized the flames were dying down. It was dark in there, darker than it was before the flames started. I got up, coughing. I stumbled to the stairs; they were hot but still intact. I didn't have time to think about how this was all possible. I didn't care about anything but getting out of there.

A few seconds later, the door at the top of the stairs opened and I used all the strength I had to rush through it. I must have caught him off guard, but I wasn't interested in looking back to catch his facial expressions or anything. I fumbled my way through the house until I found the front door. Once I got out, I just ran. And ran. And ran. Until I passed out."

I quickly tapped the stop button. The collar of my shirt was soaked, you would have thought I had run a marathon. It was tear stained, there was probably a bit of sweat there too. I wasn't sure if I was crying for Jacory, after hearing what this man had been through; hearing the cracks in his voice as he tried to keep his composure. I'm sure it was partly that. But more so, I knew it was because I had been played. I had been sweet talked and conned by a psychopath. The realization that had we been in the real world, I may very well have been one of his victims was almost too much to bear. I was a combination of grateful and mortified. Nothing had happened to me. He hadn't touched me, seduced me, he hadn't done anything to me physically. Yet I felt violated. I felt like if mental rape was a thing, that's what I had been.

I cried for about fifteen minutes. Crocodile tears and loud sobs. It was a feeling I didn't think I could shake. I sent an email immediately to my professor, letting her know I would not be returning to that internship assignment. That was all I said. I didn't even care if it delayed my graduation. It was obvious that years of studying the behaviors linked to the human brain had taught me nothing. I'd figure that out later though. I stared at the screen for a while before going back to the search page. I scrolled through more articles about Lebannon Smith. I don't know why I felt the need to torture myself with knowing more, but I couldn't not know.

From what I could piece together, Lebannon did indeed snap after his long-term girlfriend had been caught cheating on him during his final year of college. She was his first victim. There were small fragments of teeth left throughout the bottom of the basement, allowing for many identifications. There were plenty of families that got some sort of closure, but there were still so many who had not.

The number was only estimated. Lebannon never did give the authorities an accurate answer on how many there had been. He was the one who lead them to believe the number surpassed one hundred. They were only able to successfully link seventy-two missing persons to him and his blue basement.

I looked at the clock and realized I had been down the Lebannon Smith rabbit hole for hours. It didn't matter though; I didn't have to be up early anymore. I wasn't going back to the asylum. I'd figure out what to do whenever I did wake up.

Just as I was about to shut the laptop, I noticed another article. It made me so sad. I was overwhelmed with a sudden guilt and desperation. Jacory had been sharing his experience with as many people as he could, but apparently, he couldn't handle it anymore. The stress of it all eventually led him to a total mental breakdown. His family announced the cancellation of his remaining speaking engagements. He had been committed to a mental facility in order to help him heal and regain his mental health. Henry Ellin Asylum was where his family reported him being committed, asking for peace as Jacory dealt with his mental health.

They committed him to Henry Ellin Asylum. They committed him to the same mental facility with the man who had tried to kill him. Jacory wasn't crazy. He wasn't delusional. He was petrified. I didn't want to, but I had to go back. I had to get him out of there and away from that man. Before it was too late.

Be on the lookout for "The Watchtower."

ABOUT THE AUTHOR

Felicia couldn't be more excited about her debut thriller. Having been writing stories since she was in elementary school, she has finally allowed herself to take use her writing as a form of entertainment for others. Growing up in Milledgeville, GA she won many writing contests over the years, now that she is an adult, she works hard to ensure her writing is award winning.

As the CEO of Hustle Write Publication LLC, Felicia dedicates her energy not just to writing her own work to entertain, she also ghostwrites for others to get their testimonies out for those who need to hear. Her company offers not only writing services, but a blog filled with tips, tricks, ideas, and prompts for indie authors to help ensure their works are successful.

Behind the Blue Elevator is something Felicia is very proud of, and looks forward to reading your reviews on platforms such as Amazon and iBooks. She also encourages follows on business social media accounts and subscriptions to her website www.hustlewritepublication.com to stay up to date on future releases, and special insider information.